I0665965

ON THE
EDGE

ON THE EDGE

A MACKENZIE PRENTICE MYSTERY

MARY PIERCE

Seven Windows LLC

Copyright © 2024 by Mary Pierce
All rights reserved.
ISBN: 979-8-9881776-5-4

No part of this publication may be reproduced, distributed, or transmitted in any form or by any means, including photocopying, recording, or other electronic or mechanical methods, without the prior written permission of the publisher, except as permitted by US copyright law. For permission requests, contact infosevenwindowsllc@gmail.com.

The story, all names, characters, and incidents portrayed in this production are fictitious. No identification with actual persons (living or deceased), places, buildings, and products is intended or should be inferred.

Book design and editing by Michelle Rayburn (missionandmedia.com)
Cover art by Mary Pierce

First edition 2024

Sisters function as safety nets in a chaotic world
simply by being there for each other.

—Carol Saline, *Sisters*

A sister is a little bit of childhood that can never be lost.

—Marion C. Garretty

For my dear sister Carol

CHAPTER ONE

Tuesday, June 25, 10:30 a.m.

THE PAST IS THE past. Things buried back there should stay buried. No such luck. It's hard enough to figure out who did what yesterday. How was I supposed to figure out what happened over twenty years ago?

I was in middle school when fifteen-year-old Maisie Gordon went over the cliff above the Wolf River and smashed onto the rocks below.

The cliff has a huge "3R" that someone carved into the face of the rock decades ago. I've pictured whoever it was rappelling over the edge to chisel away at the cliff face. That's the how. But why? Maybe Mount Rushmore inspired them. Whoever has the answer is probably long gone. The who and the why of the 3R carving remain a mystery.

The official ruling on Maisie Gordon's death was suicide. Now her mother was in the chair next to my desk in the reception area at TriMak Investigations, looking for help.

I work here ten-to-four, five days a week, more or less. I set my own hours. I'm the office manager for now and partners with Trip Kipling and the retired chief of the Three Rivers Police Department, Chief Bronson. So far, my snooping has been semi-official—invited to do so by family or friends—while I'm waiting for my investigator's license. I took the state exam and hope to be officially snooping soon.

Mrs. Gordon was rail thin, and her skin had a gray pallor. "I'm not well," she said, tapping her chest. "Lung cancer. Stage four. Metastatic."

"I'm so sorry," I said.

She told me the cancer had been there, off and on, for three years. "I've tried to stay positive, but now it's back with a vengeance. I know I don't have much time left."

I opened a file on my laptop and typed as she talked. "They said it was suicide, and I begged them to do more investigating, but they said there was no reason to do that."

"Did Maisie leave a note?"

"Yes, but I didn't accept it." She stopped, stared at the floor, took a wheezing, shuddering breath, and met my eyes. "The note just said, 'It's all too much.' That could mean anything, couldn't it?" She coughed into a Kleenex, then breathed again, with great effort, before continuing. "Too much pressure at school. Too much money for a pair of jeans. Who knows what she meant?"

Another cough. Another gasping breath. "If she was going to end her life, she would have said, 'I can't take it anymore, and I'm sorry. I love you, but it's just too much,' or something like that."

I nodded. "Yes, but in a lot of cases, there's no note at all."

She slumped back in the chair. "That doesn't make it easier. If she hadn't left that note, maybe the police would have done more. But since that note was there, they just assumed she'd taken her own life."

I felt bad for Mrs. Gordon. A mother with a dead daughter who left a note, but not the kind of note her mother wanted. A mother who needed closure, especially now, when her time was short.

Mrs. Gordon went on. "I've never believed my daughter would do that. She was so happy, always smiling. Light in heart and spirit, you know?" She paused, smiled. "Her name—Maisie—means 'wished for.' Her father wanted a boy and tried to cover his disappointment when a second daughter was born. I named her Maisie so she would always know I wanted her, even if he wasn't thrilled."

"That's sweet," I said.

My name, Mackenzie, means "fire-born." That fits, after the recent cornfield incident. And the fire in my apartment. My name also means "good-looking," but the jury is out on that. I'm not gorgeous, but I'm kind of cute. My grandmother says I'm a "just-right, Goldilocks kind of girl." At five-six, not too tall, not too short. Not too fat, not too skinny. At thirty-five, not too young, not too old. I have cool green eyes and decent brownish hair. I have a good sense of humor, and I'm pretty smart.

And modest, Snarky Me added.

Mrs. Gordon reached for a fresh tissue from the box on my desk. She pressed her right hand against her heart and closed her eyes. With effort, she took another breath, which ignited a coughing spasm. She leaned forward, coughing into the tissue several times.

I winced. It sounded so painful.

At last, she sat up and wiped her mouth with the tissue.

"Can I get you some water?" I asked.

She shook her head. "I'm okay. I just want to know for sure what happened to my baby. That's why I'm here. I just need to know."

This was a mother's almost-deathbed request. Who could refuse that? "Tell me about Maisie," I said.

Maisie Gordon had just finished her sophomore year at Three Rivers High. She played clarinet in the band and was a good student. Mrs. Gordon pulled a photo from her purse, a five-by-seven of the three of them—Mom, Maisie, and her older sister, Charity. Smiling together. They wore matching necklaces—crosses with a stone at the center of each. "I got us matching necklaces for Christmas that year. See?" She lifted the cross from her neck and held it toward me. "Mine is a sapphire for December." The blue stone glinted in the office light.

"Very pretty," I said.

She pointed at the picture. "Maisie's is a ruby. She was born on the Fourth of July. Charity was born just before Thanksgiving." She pointed at the yellowish stone. "Hers is a topaz."

"Very pretty," I said again, feeling a little envious. My single, working mother never had extra money to buy her daughters that kind of thing.

Mrs. Gordon put the photo back in her purse and sighed. "Maisie's necklace got lost. I'd love to have it now. And Charity says it's too painful to wear hers. Too many memories." She blew her nose. "I'll take that water now if you don't mind."

I went to the kitchen in the back of the office and got a bottle of water from the fridge. When I returned, Mrs. Gordon's eyes were closed.

"Are you okay?"

She opened her eyes and nodded. "Just needed a moment." She tried to twist the cap off the bottle without success. "Oh, for God's sake!"

"Let me do that for you," I said and opened it.

She took a long swallow, eyes closed. She let out a breath, opened her eyes, and set the bottle down. "What else do you need to know?"

In response to my questions, Mrs. Gordon told me that Maisie had two close girlfriends in high school. She spelled their names for me.

I typed JEMMA DALWORTHY and ONYX LYDEN into my laptop. According to Maisie's mother, neither friend thought anything was wrong in Maisie's life, no reason to suspect she was depressed or unhappy. Certainly, no reason to kill herself.

"Did Maisie have a boyfriend?"

I waited through another coughing episode. Mrs. Gordon took a sip of water, then said, "No, but she wrote a heart on her bedroom mirror with a capital B in the middle. I've left it there. I've left her whole room as it was. I just couldn't bring myself to clear it out. I assume she had a crush, but no, she never dated anyone. I've read through her diary. No mention of any boys."

She pulled a small, spiral-bound journal from her purse and handed it to me. "Here. Maybe you'll see something in it that I didn't." The journal had a bunch of kittens on the cover.

"Maisie loved cats," she said, smiling. "We had three of them at the time, all from the same litter. I said we could have just one, but the girls begged to take all three. I couldn't say no. Maisie named them Snap, Crackle, and Pop. Adorable." The last word drifted away.

I smiled. "That's cute. I have a cat myself. I get it." Chloe had adopted me as her human after my apartment was firebombed. She and I live—temporarily, I tell myself—at my grandmother's Victorian house.

"That's another reason I know she didn't do this intentionally. All three of those cats slept with her. She never would have abandoned them." Mrs. Gordon went quiet as I added to my notes.

After another sip of water, she said, "Her older sister, Charity, was a senior that year. She's a doctor now. Did I mention that?"

I shook my head. "I'll need to talk with Charity. Does she work here in town?"

"Yes. She's at the clinic at Our Lady of Mercy. She's Charity Carson now, married to Zach." She looked at me as if I should know who he was.

I drew a blank. "Who is Zach?"

"Zachary Carson. Judge Carson's son."

Ah. Charity had married into one of the most prominent families in town. Judge Rollo Carson was a good friend of Chief Bronson's and well-respected in Three Rivers.

Mrs. Gordon said, "I'd hoped for grandchildren but Charity's so focused on her career she's never had time for babies." She coughed twice, then continued. "Charity took Maisie's death very hard. Blamed herself. Said she should have been able to tell." She paused, tears welling. She wiped her eyes. "I think that's why she became a doctor. To save others."

"Very noble," I said. "What about your husband? Maisie's dad?"

"He died when the girls were young. An accident at work. The company was negligent." She'd lost her husband. Her children had no father.

I could relate. My father left one night to get cigarettes and never came back. At the time, we lived in The City a couple hours west of Three Rivers. My mother decided that the big city was no place for her to be a single mother. She moved us five kids (I'm the middle one.) to Three Rivers to be closer to Gram and the rest of the family. Best decision ever, if you ask me.

"We got a huge financial settlement, but that doesn't make up for losing your husband, your father. Charity was seven, and Maisie was five. They barely even remembered their dad."

She took another tissue and blew her nose. I looked out the front window of the office, thinking about girls and their fathers. Wondering where mine might be. Alive? Dead? No clue.

She continued. "I did my best. I had to be mom and dad—the dance lessons, showing up for every soccer game, every band concert. Maisie played clarinet. Did I mention that? The three of us girls made it on our own. We did just fine. Well, we were fine until Maisie—" She swallowed hard and leaned closer, making direct eye contact. Intense. "You *have* to help me. I *have* to know what happened."

I leaned back in my chair. "It's been a long time, Mrs. Gordon. I'm not sure where to even start. And what if the answer is the same?"

"I just need to know for certain. To know that I've done everything I could to be sure."

"Have you talked to the police?"

"The police wouldn't do anything back then, and they sure won't do anything now." She reached out and clasped my arm. "Please help me. Hiring your agency is my only hope."

I felt a clench in my gut. What if I failed to figure this one out? The chief and Trip might say we'd be nuts to take it on. It had been so long.

I looked into Mrs. Gordon's eyes and saw the pain. Deep sorrow. Desperate longing.

A mother's dying wish.

"Okay. We'll see what we can do."

She grabbed my hand with both of hers. "Thank you. Thank you," she said.

I'd given her hope, and I hoped that it would not be in vain.

CHAPTER TWO

MRS. GORDON LEFT. I needed coffee. I think better when caffeinated. The office coffeemaker—a one-cup-at-a-time machine with a hot water reservoir—is in the back room between the small refrigerator and the sink.

I insisted on this kind of coffee maker since when I worked for Trip before, at the financial services office, I had to make the coffee every day. I didn't want that to be the case at TriMak. Everybody makes their own around here, not just "the girl."

I thought about Maisie as I waited for my cup of donut shop coffee to brew. Fifteen. Sweet girl. Happy. Cat lover. Why would she decide she had no reason to live? On the surface, she seemed fine, but I remembered my own teenage angst.

I'd fallen madly in love with my late ex, Billy, in high school. We had breakups and makeups. Typical teen drama. Later, I married him, then divorced him. Then he ended up dead, and I figured out how that happened. And that's how I ended up working at TriMak and solving puzzles. Funny the turns life takes.

Solving puzzles—mysteries—is like a real-life game of Clue. Who did what to whom, where, when, and how. And in Maisie's case—why?

I love that kind of stuff. Puzzles. Logic problems. And I love math. Love the fact that one plus one is always two. There are reasons for things, and I can dig to find those reasons. When things don't add up, I want to know why.

As I carried my coffee back to my desk, I felt a familiar determination growing with each step. Badass Me was on the case. *Yes, Mrs. Gordon, I will help you. Yes, Maisie, I will figure this one out.*

Rational Me stepped in. *Where the heck do we even start?*

I continued the list in my computer: Talk to the chief. Chief Bronson was sure to have some insight. He hadn't come into the office yet this morning. Maybe I could catch him this afternoon.

I added Maisie's sister, Charity, to the list with Jemma and Onyx.

Who else? Anyone who knew her back then. Who were her teachers? Yearbooks could help with that. Did she see a school counselor? A therapist? Those records would be confidential and likely destroyed after all this time.

I added Heather Sullivan to the list. Heather is a detective with Three Rivers PD and worked with Billy. She was also one of the women he slept with. Billy "dating" other women was the reason our marriage ended.

Heather had apologized—made amends to me as part of her AA recovery—and I'd forgiven her. Billy was dead. No point in holding on to old hurts.

Heather and I'd had close encounters of the professional kind over the last year or so. Some cordial, but some contentious. We'd recently come to an understanding of mutual respect, on my part at least, and a willingness to share information to the extent that Heather could do so.

In the Gordon case, Heather could help me find copies of the paperwork and maybe help me track down the people who worked the case, if they were still around.

I sat back, feeling good. I had some sense of the first steps I might take in The Tragic Case of Maisie Gordon. I was tempted to call it that, but that sounded like one of those Perry Mason episodes my grandmother loves to watch on the *Murders and Mysteries* channel.

Snarky Me whispered, *Sounds more Sherlock Holmes-y to me. Who do you think you are?*

I shook off that thought and named the file the boring way, with the date and Maisie's name.

I was ready to start my investigation when an alarm on my phone went off. Eleven forty-five. Lunchtime. Snooping would have to wait.

CHAPTER THREE

I LOCKED THE OFFICE AND headed home for lunch. Four of us live together in my grandmother's Victorian house. My mother moved in a few years back after selling her house to help Gram care for her third husband, Nathan. I moved in last fall.

Gram and Nathan are both in their eighties, and Nathan has started forgetting things. "Losing my marbles," is how he puts it.

Gram had asked me to come home to sit with Nathan for a couple hours while she went to Ivy's Cut & Curl for a perm.

I parked behind the house and went inside. Gram's cheery yellow and green kitchen was as hot and humid as the air outside.

Nathan was at the table slurping a bowl of Gram's home-made chicken noodle soup. I patted his shoulder. "Kind of hot for soup, isn't it?"

He looked up and squinted at me. "Evelyn! Where've you been?"

He sometimes calls me by his late wife's name. Usually I ignore it, but since he and I would be hanging out together, I corrected him.

"No, I'm Mackenzie."

He looked surprised. "Well, nice of you to stop by. How do we know each other?"

I explained again how I was the granddaughter of his wife, Virginia. I reminded him that I live with him, Gram, and my mother. I didn't go into detail about the apartment fire that had forced me to move here. Or how I couldn't wait to move into the carriage house behind the Victorian, once it was renovated.

I just patted his arm and said I was glad to hang out with him for a few hours. I popped two pieces of Gram's cranberry wild rice bread into the toaster on the counter and sat at the table. "How are you doing today, Nathan?"

He looked up from the soup. "I think I need to go see my mother."

His mother had died decades ago. Gram says we should all just go along with Nathan. "It's his reality of the moment," she says. Not telling him again that his mother was gone or that his brother had died. "Reminding him is cruel," Gram says, "inviting the grief to return over and over again."

I said, "Sure, Nathan, maybe we can do that later. We'll see how the weather is. Storm warnings out there."

Our local weather guy—oops, I mean meteorologist—is a cheerful little fellow named Stuart Klump. (No weather people going by fancy names like Stormie Day or Dusty Rhodes around these parts.) Stuart forecasted another hot and humid day, with a chance of thunderstorms later. A typical summer forecast.

We have an endless cycle of seasons here in Three Rivers. Freezing cold and snowy with ice in winter. Hot and humid with mosquitoes in summer. We have a few days here and there that I consider "just right." No humidity, no heat. No cold, no snow. Comfortable.

I call those just-right days in the spring "ASBB," which stands for after snow, before bugs. And in the fall, after the first frost kills the mosquitoes and puts the bees to bed, we have "ABBS." After bugs, before snow.

We have just a few weeks with each. Why do we put up with it? Simple for me. I love the changes. Fall colors. The fresh crispness of early snow. The dead of winter helps me appreciate the rebirth of spring. Every season has its good stuff.

But this summer? Not so much good stuff. High heat and humidity. Thunderstorms rolling through the area. We'd had an extreme heat advisory from the National Weather Service almost every day. "Stay hydrated and check on your neighbors and the elderly," Stuart advised.

Gram's Victorian has radiators for heat and no central air conditioning. She put window units in the upstairs bedrooms, but the rest of the house can be miserable. The twelve-foot ceilings help a little since heat rises.

Nathan finished his soup and started on the bowl of home-made applesauce Gram had left for him.

My blue TriMak polo shirt stuck to my back. I stepped into the parlor, pulled the floor fan closer to the kitchen table, and sat back down.

I repeated the morning weather report. "Thunderstorms are coming."

Nathan nodded. "Not good to be driving in a thunder-storm. Did I ever tell you about the tornado?"

Ah, the oft-told tale of the tornado he experienced as a boy on the family farm in Illinois.

"No, Nathan. Tell me about it." To remind Nathan you've heard the story a bazillion times would be cruel. Pretending is kinder. Gram calls the pretense a "fiblet."

My toast popped up as Nathan retold the tale. "I was twelve. It was weather like this. Hot, sticky. And those buzzing insects, you know? Those—" he frowned, thinking hard.

"Cicadas? Is that what they are?" I buttered my toast and brought it to the table.

Nathan nodded. "Yes! Cicadas. They make such a racket, don't they?"

"Uh-huh," I said and took a bite of toast.

Nathan looked up toward the ceiling. "The clouds—I'll never forget the clouds. They turned green and then black as night. The temperature must have dropped thirty degrees in a minute. I watched from my bedroom window upstairs in the house. The cloud swirling, a huge black column of dust whirling. The tornado came straight at the house."

"That had to be so scary," I said.

"Terrifying. Fascinating and terrifying. I ran for the cellar." He paused, gave a chuckle. "My older brother—the fool—stood outside while it was coming. I screamed at him to get inside the house, but he just danced around, waving his arms, hootin' and hollerin' to beat the band. I thought sure that tornado was going to scoop him up!" He shook his head. "You know how angels protect fools? The angels protected him that day. When the tornado got close to the house, it jumped right over us. Strangest darn thing I've ever seen. Just jumped right over the house and went on."

"How weird. And how lucky you were."

Nathan nodded. "Yes, we were. The house was fine. So was my fool brother. A barn and another outbuilding were flattened.

Pieces of barnwood everywhere. We lost two cows. The others were fine, though it took a few days for them to settle down."

"How many cows did you have?"

"We had about fifty at one time. A lot of chickens. And dogs. And barn cats, of course. One of the cats had three legs. Another only had one eye. Things happen on the farm. Animals live outside. People live in the house."

"Are you okay with Chloe being inside here?"

He looked puzzled. "Chloe?"

"My cat. Chloe. With the black-and-white stripes?" She must have heard her name because she chose that moment to walk into the kitchen. "Speak of the devil," I said. I picked her up.

Nathan reached a hand forward. "Hi, kitty."

Chloe purred and bent her head for petting. "She likes you," I said.

"The feeling's mutual," Nathan said, scratching her behind the ears.

I set Chloe on the floor, and Nathan and I finished lunch, chatting about pets and weather and life on the farm. This is how it was with Nathan. He quickly forgets current happenings but has clear and vivid memories of his childhood. Every once in a while, he comes up with a story I've never heard before.

After lunch, I suggested we take a walk around the block before Nathan took his usual post-lunch snooze. I helped him put on his sneakers, changed from sandals into my ASICs, and we headed out the front door.

The humid air felt heavy as a blanket as we walked. I kept pace with Nathan. It's hard when you are in your thirties to walk like you're in your eighties. Snails could have passed us.

The neighbor's cat—a calico named Misty—followed us for a bit. Two yards had dogs behind fences. The dachshund barked a warning. The German shepherd wagged a welcome.

As we went around the block, I kept the conversation going, commenting on how big the neighbor's hydrangeas were getting.

"They love this weather," Nathan said.

I told him that Mrs. Esposito at the end of the block had applied to raise chickens, a new thing in town.

"Annoying buggers," Nathan said. "They belong in the country, not the city. Don't need a rooster waking everyone up."

He told me—a story I'd not heard—how they had a rooster on the farm that crowed constantly. "Something was seriously wrong with that bugger," he said.

"Well, roosters gotta crow, don't they?"

"Not like he did. My brother took care of him."

"How?"

"Twenty-two," Nathan said solemnly.

I swear I heard taps being played. Poor rooster.

CHAPTER FOUR

NATHAN WAS NAPPING WHEN Gram got home from her hair appointment just before two-thirty. I gave her a hug and headed to the office.

Trip and the chief were both in the chief's office when I got back to TriMak. I paused at the open door.

Trip leaned over the desk as Chief Bronson explained how to tie the fishing fly on the stand in front of him. "Just wrap this around here. Like that. See?"

I cleared my throat. They both looked at me.

The chief smiled. "Come on in, Chickie!" He started calling me Chickie a while back after he said I was "madder than a wet hen." At first, I hated the name, but now I find it, well, endearing, for lack of a better word. "I was just showing young Trip here how things are done."

Trip bent forward, palms together. "Ah yes, sensei. I bow to your expertise."

The chief nodded. "Wise choice, young Trip. Wise choice."

Trip is older than I am—he's forty-four—and until recently, he lived under his father's shadow. Trip's dad, known around town as Big George, is a hard man. Trip and I worked together at Big George's financial services company until Trip's dad fired him and closed the business.

Trip decided to forge his own path and opened TriMak, with the chief and me as his partners. Trip's licensed as an investigator but spends much of his time promoting the business around the area. He and the chief golf every Wednesday morning with a group of the town's movers and shakers, and they trade off attending local meetings with the Lions, the Elks, and the Moose.

That's great for the two of them. I just want to solve the puzzles, not waste my time schmoozing.

Since opening TriMak, the tension Trip carried when he worked for his dad has disappeared. He's different now. Night and day different. He is jovial, comes to work whistling. I like Trip 2.0.

Nothing romantic, of course. He's not my type. Not. At. All. He's okay looking but a little too paunchy for me. He wears his sandy hair longish, I assume to compensate for the balding on top. He's not at the comb-over stage yet, thank goodness. And he's too rich. We both grew up here, but we travel in completely different circles.

Trip went to fancy, private schools. I'm public school.

He grew up in the country club set and took European vacations in the summer. I spent my summers at the municipal pool.

He's silver spoon. I'm plastic spork.

You get the picture.

I took the extra chair in front of the chief's desk. Trip sat back in his chair, then took a bite of a jelly-filled Bismarck. A glob of jelly squirted onto his shirt. He looked down, wiped the jelly on his finger. His hair flopped into his face. He lifted his hand to shove his hair off his forehead.

I'd seen this before with Trip. I tried to warn him. "You have jelly—" I pointed.

Too late. Jelly gooped into his hair and streaked the bald spot on top of his head.

He realized what he'd done. "Oh, crap," he said. He dipped his sticky fingers into his coffee and rubbed his hair. He sucked the jelly off his fingers, rinsed them in his coffee, and then dried his hand on the inside of his TriMak polo shirt.

The chief and I watched, enraptured. And disgusted.

When Trip had finished cleaning himself, the chief said, "We were just discussing my fishing trip." This is an annual trip the chief takes with three of his friends.

Chief Bronson is in his sixties and loves being semi-retired, setting his own schedule, taking off whenever he feels like it. He's a silent partner in our agency, working behind the scenes. He's in and out, often in disguise since he is a very recognizable figure in town.

He cast an imaginary line over his head and reeled it in. "Leaving next week, right after the Fourth. Can't wait." He turned to me. "Did you need something, Chickie?"

I filled them in on the Gordon case. "Is it okay with you guys if I run with this one?"

The chief frowned. "Don't know that you'll be able to change anything. You can request the paperwork, assuming it's still available. Paper copies may be floating around. Photos of the scene, maybe. Some of those old files might still be on site in the basement of the department. We were scanning old files before I left. Of course, some files were destroyed in the fire."

A fire in the old courthouse in downtown Three Rivers twenty years or so ago had destroyed a large part of the landmark building. The police department was housed there at the time. After the fire, the PD moved to a more central location on Lake Street and First Avenue, just south of downtown.

Trip double-checked his hands to be sure he was jelly-free, then leaned back in his chair and crossed his arms over his stomach. "It will be good practice for you while you're waiting for your license."

I held up crossed fingers. "Any day now, I hope." Then I'd be official and could take on any case I wanted. No more asking for permission from the chief or Trip.

Trip added, "Just don't step on any toes."

The chief said, "Trip, Mackenzie appreciates our relationships with the powers that be. She understands how important it is to tread lightly around police matters. She won't be jeopardizing the agency. Or screwing things up for herself." He turned to me and winked. "You're too smart for that, aren't you, Chickie?"

I assured them both how smart I was and headed to my desk. I was thinking about my next steps in the Gordon case when the front door opened. A wave of heat followed a little girl into the reception area.

She looked about seven—my niece Violet's age. She wore a pink-and-yellow-flowered sundress over black shorts and blue jelly shoes. Her brown hair was pulled into pigtails, and she wore pink-framed glasses. She was carrying an empty birdcage.

I smiled. She smiled back, revealing spaces where her front teeth had been.

"Is this the detective place?" She had a little lisp. Adorable.

"Yes. Is your mommy with you?"

"She's parking the car."

"What's your name, sweetie?"

"Louisa."

"How can I help you, Louisa?"

"Banjo is missing."

"You lost your banjo?"

Her lip trembled. "Yes. He flew away this morning."

Ah. "What kind of bird is he?"

"He's a blue parakeet, about this big." She showed me with her fingers. "Can you find him?" She pulled a crumpled dollar out of a pocket and set it on the counter. "I can pay you from my allowance."

Her mother walked in just then. "Louisa, I told you to wait while I parked the car."

"I couldn't wait, Mommy. We have to find Banjo."

The mother looked at me. "I'm so sorry, but she insisted we come here. She reads every sign around town, and when we passed your office the other day, she sounded out the word *investigations,* and I explained what you do here. Then, when the bird went missing, she insisted we come. I'm so sorry. I'm sure you have more important things to do. Come along, Louisa."

Louisa stamped her foot, glared at her mother. "No! She can help! I'm not leaving." She threw herself down on the tile of the reception area.

I stood and looked over the counter at her. "Louisa, Banjo could be all the way to Mexico by now. Hanging out with the parrots in the jungle. He could be happy there."

She glared at me, then stuck out her lower lip. "But maybe he's not. Maybe he's just lost." She stood up, came to the counter, and put her little hands on it. Tears rimmed her lower lids. Her lip trembled. "Can't you help? Please?"

Second tearful request of the morning. I looked at Louisa's mother.

She said, "I'll be happy to pay you for your time."

"No, it's fine." I handed the dollar back. I could not, in good conscience, take money for this one. "I'll take a look around and see if I can find Banjo." I jotted their name, address, and phone number on a yellow sticky note. "I'll let you know what I find."

Louisa's mother grabbed her by the arm and marched her out of the office. I overheard the mother saying, "Now, don't get your hopes up, Louisa." Wise advice.

Two cases. Great start to the week. At least TriMak would get paid for one of them.

We could have gotten paid for both if I'd taken the kid's dollar.

CHAPTER FIVE

THE CHIEF AND TRIP had left for the day, and just before five, I locked the office and headed to Sully's Gym, near downtown in what used to be Otto's Meat Market. I work out at Sully's three times a week, usually Tuesday and Thursday after work and again on Saturday mornings. Sometimes less. Sometimes not at all.

When I say I "work out," I mean I'm trying to build some strength. The chief strongly recommended I do so and hooked me up with his personal trainer, a tall Norwegian named Gustaf.

Three other women—Michelle, Stacy, and Yolanda—and I are known as Gustaf's Gang. The other three are actually preparing for a bodybuilding competition later this fall. Posing nearly naked is not for me. I'm just trying to build some muscle and keep the chief off my case.

I changed into my gym clothes, locked my locker, and headed into the weight room. Michelle was working her biceps with twenty-five-pound weights. Yolanda was hoisting herself up on the chinning bar. Stacy wasn't there.

"Where's Stace?" I asked.

"Her little boy's sick," Yolanda managed between reps.

I picked up the ten-pounders and joined the grunting. "Were you guys around when Maisie Gordon died?"

Michelle frowned. "Who?"

I told the story.

Yolanda said, "I remember that. I was in elementary school, like third grade, but my big brother was in high school. I remember him talking about it at the dinner table."

Michelle nodded. "Yeah, I remember something about that. Why you asking?"

"I've been hired to investigate."

Yolanda frowned. "What's to investigate? She killed herself, didn't she?"

I stopped lifting. "That's the official word, but her family wants to know if that's what really happened. Do you remember anything at all?"

Yolanda stepped back from the chinning bar. "I worked with her friend at the hospital—a nurse with a weird name."

"Onyx?"

She brightened. "Yeah, that's it. Onyx Lyden. I remember her talking about it."

"Do you remember what she said?"

Yolanda thought a moment, then said, "Onyx said how sad it was that the girl died. And she couldn't understand how the girl was so sweet, but her sister—Doctor Carson is her sister—could be such a you-know-what." She shook her head. "She's a good doctor, I guess, but she treated us nurses like crap. Like we were her slaves."

"So you don't remember Onyx saying anything about Maisie's death?"

She shook her head. "No. Just how sad it was. You'd think her sister would be nicer to people after going through something like that."

We finished working out, chatting about the upcoming competition, the guys in our lives, what a tyrant Gustaf could be. The usual girl talk.

I left the gym and headed home, thinking about Maisie's sister, Charity. She'd become a doctor. Her sister's death had motivated her to try to save others. That spoke of compassion. And maybe she just had an abrupt manner at work. Some people are all business.

CHAPTER SIX

AFTER SEVEN ON TUESDAY night, I was drying dishes at Gram's. I watched the evening sky through the window over the sink. Dark clouds gathered. Distant thunder rumbled.

Gram had made lasagna, and I'd had two big servings of its four-layered scrumptiousness.

Lasagna is our reward for that strenuous workout. Rational Me loves a good rationalization.

Snarky had other thoughts. *Strenuous? A dozen curls with ten-pound weights? Hardly!* If Snarky had her way, I'd never be able to eat lasagna again.

I'd volunteered for cleanup duty. Part of me finds dishwashing and cleanup oh-so-very-satisfying. Getting the kitchen back to clean and pristine feels good.

Gram and Nathan had headed for bed upstairs. Definitely in the early-to-bed-early-to-rise club.

My mother was at the dining room table working on her laptop. She swore. Loudly.

"Something wrong in there?" I called as I draped the dish-towel over the oven door handle, adjusting the edges evenly, then smoothing it with my palms. Little-Bit-of-OCD Me smiled. *Ahh.*

My mother hollered, "Ugh! I give up!"

I stood in the dining room doorway as she snapped the laptop closed and slammed her hand against the table.

She'd recently lost her job at Lumber City Bank when that bank decided to merge with Tri-State Bank. My mother was caught on the wrong side of their rightsizing.

She'd been at the computer for days, updating her résumé and looking online for a new job.

Three Rivers isn't the big city, but we do have jobs. And my mother has a lot of bookkeeping experience. She worked in the business office of the local shoe factory when I was in high school.

A fringe benefit of that job was meeting Duncan, the man she's been dating since they reconnected last fall. *What do we call him? Her boyfriend? Partner? Significant other? Love interest? Boy toy? Ew.*

She scowled. "Why am I even looking? I'm sixty-two. Who is going to hire me over someone younger, fresh out of school, who knows all the technical stuff? I've tried to keep up, but things are changing so fast. Good grief! I remember when you had to actually *dial* a phone. I'm like a dinosaur in today's job market."

Gram had come downstairs in her robe just in time to hear that. She piped up. "Geez Louise! If you're a dinosaur, what does that make me?"

"You're not even air-breathing yet," my mother said.

Gram sighed. "I'm just a blob in the primordial ooze." She put her hands toward me, fingers wiggling. "Watch out! Here comes the blob!"

I stepped back and laughed. "Go blob all over somebody else!"

Gram chuckled. "I'm glad I don't have to worry about competing out there. Not that I ever did. All I ever did was take care of the family and the house."

I said, "Most important job ever, Gram. We're all grateful you were there. *Always* there."

My mom got huffy. "Well, I would have been there if your father—"

I held up my hand. "Nothing personal, Mother. Don't even go there."

My mother often complained about how different her life would have been if my father had stuck around. His disappearance was a mystery. I'd thought often about him when I was younger, wondering where he'd gone, if he was still living. Now it was just easier to think he might be dead than to think he was alive and well out there somewhere but didn't care enough about us to ever come back.

Gram hugged my mother around the shoulders. "Barbara, you did a great job raising your family. I'm proud of you, honey."

"It wasn't easy."

Gram patted my mother on the back. "I know. It's the hardest thing, raising children alone. But like they say, the bigger the challenge, the better the story." She gave me a triumphant nod. "I read that on Facebook."

My mom scoffed. "Yeah, yeah. But the trick is to survive your story."

Gram said, "It's not what happens to you, but it's what you tell yourself about it. You lose somebody or lose your job, you tell yourself it's hopeless and give up. Or you can tell yourself to keep on going."

Wise, my grandmother. I said, "You've never given up, Mom. You raised us. You've worked hard. You're resilient. And you'll get through this."

She shook her head and sighed. "I'm not so sure. I just saw something—probably on Facebook—that said, 'When it feels like it's all too much, it is.' That's how I feel right now. No job. No future. It's all too much." She stood. "I'm going to bed."

As she left the room, a boom of thunder shook the house. The dining room lights flickered. An electric charge filled the air. I rubbed my forearms and hugged myself.

"That was a big one," Gram said. "I'd better go check on Nathan. Good night again, sweetie." She headed back upstairs.

I poured a glass of lemonade from the pitcher in the fridge, thinking. "It's all too much," my mother had said. Maisie Gordon had said the same thing in her note. What had she meant?

Mrs. Gordon had sought my help. She just wanted to know—for certain—what happened. I hoped I could find Maisie's missing necklace for her. It might have fallen off when Maisie fell. Or she could have lost it anywhere. Someone may have found it and kept it. It might be lost forever. But I would do all I could to find it.

Mrs. Gordon wasn't giving up. Neither was I.

CHAPTER SEVEN

TOOK MY LEMONADE OUTSIDE and sat on Gram's back porch steps. The storm would be on us very soon. The day had been stifling hot. The wind was chilly now, a welcome relief after the day's heat. Lightning flashed in the distance, accompanied by an almost constant drumroll of thunder.

I looked over at the carriage house at the back of Gram's large lot. She'd hired Milcross Builders a couple months before to redo the exterior of her Victorian. The main house has had several owners over its life. A previous owner had altered the exterior and disqualified the old house—built in the Civil War era—from the Three Rivers historic home registry. Gram hadn't minded in the past. "I wouldn't want to end up on some house tour with a bunch of strangers traipsing in and out."

But then, last winter, she saw pictures of the San Francisco Victorians known as the Painted Ladies and decided she wanted her home to be like those. She was even open to opening the house for tours, which I was pretty sure my anxious mother would hate.

The project had been going well for the last several weeks. Updated exterior paint in soft green for the siding, trimmed in a warm white with brick red for the accents. Lots of lovely detail on the corbels and cornices, eaves, and gingerbread. The porch railing that wraps around two sides of the front of the house had been meticulously repaired. The porch swing—a favorite thinking and dreaming spot of mine growing up—had been updated with fresh paint, and its overhead beam had been reinforced.

An adjunct project involved converting the carriage house on the back of Gram's lot into housing for yours truly. I have to admit, it was not the least bit unpleasant to have to talk about the project with Nick Milcross. I'd known Nick since high school, where he was cool and I was, um, less than cool. The girls loved him. The boys admired him. He's tall, just over six feet, and athletic, with wavy brown hair and velvety brown eyes. And he has dimples.

I'd spent a lot of time with Nick lately discussing flooring, paint colors, interior trim choices, and appliance placement. (All on Gram's dime. She insists. What can I do?)

So many decisions to make. So many opportunities to be close to Nick, to inhale the scent of him—a mix of soap and Old Spice—with a little good old-fashioned, hard-working-man sweat.

I told my yoga-guru friend Tansy one day that I loved how Nick smelled. "Man sweat. Nothing better," I said.

"Seriously?"

I shrugged. "What can I say?"

She looked at me. "Ew. That's what I say."

"He wears Old Spice, and I like that. Reminds me of my grandfather, Papa Powell."

"That's better. Old Spice is nice," Tansy said.

Nick's a gentle guy. He's kind and patient. He loves his parents. He hangs out with his grandfather, the founder of three-generation Milcross Builders. He visits his grandma at Drury's Rest. He has a great laugh. I'd felt an attraction last spring when we danced together, and that attraction had grown stronger over the past weeks.

Rational Me knows it is too soon to say I'm falling in love. Anxious Me recommends caution. I've been disappointed in the past—by a cheating husband and by guys who say they'll call and then don't. I'm not in any hurry to risk more hurt. Although Lonely Me thinks it's stupid to wait.

But then again, Nick Milcross isn't making any moves. He's not asking for any commitments.

And besides, there's the question of Vince Hampton.

Firefighter, like my older brother Greg. Friend and high school classmate of Greg's and object of my middle school crush. Our relationship—if you can even call it that—had a rough start. He'd asked me out, but then I saw him with his ex-wife a couple times. I jumped to conclusions that turned out to be completely incorrect. Score one for my anxiety.

Brother Greg butted in and told Vince I liked him. Vince called. We'd gone out a couple of times.

Vince is very different from Nick. If they were in a western, Nick would be wearing a white hat, Vince a black one. Not that Vince isn't a stand-up guy, but there's an edge to him.

Nick is open-hearted, honest, kind, and gentle. Predictable, reliable.

Vince is, well, more of a wild card.

Maybe it's the line of work for each of them. Nick builds things with his father and grandfather. He is the kind of guy who helps old ladies cross the street. He's soft-spoken and sweet.

He takes his time, thinks things through, and he's not afraid to share a feeling.

Vince runs into burning buildings. He drives fast, lives fast. He's been known to drink too much, which I can relate to. He's divorced. He may or may not still love his ex-wife, who recently moved out of town. You can't be sure where you stand with Vince.

Nick doesn't drink. He goes to church with his family on Sundays. Has dinner with his parents on a regular basis. Never married. He's faithful, clean, and reverent. A real Boy Scout.

Vince doesn't always follow the rules, and he smells like smoke and bourbon.

If forced to choose between the two, I couldn't. Something in each of them appeals to something in me.

Lonely Me finds reliable and faithful appealing. She is a hundred percent Team Nick.

Badass Me likes a challenge and excitement. Team Vince, no question.

Anxious Me sounds the Klaxon Horn. *Ahooga! Love equals pain! Danger! Neither! Run!*

Snarky Me, well, snarks. *Oh, for cryin' out loud, date them both! See what happens.*

It's so crowded in my head at times.

Lightning struck so close I felt the electric charge. A crack of thunder followed immediately. Every part of me knew it was time to get inside. A heavy rain started before I even shut the back door.

CHAPTER EIGHT

Wednesday, June 26

WEDNESDAY DAWNED BRIGHT AND clear. Another hot day was on tap. I got into the office just after ten, ready to start working on the Gordon case. I called Mrs. Gordon. Yes, she had the yearbook from Charity's senior year, which was Maisie's sophomore year. I could stop by anytime to pick it up.

Mrs. Gordon lives on the West Hill, an area of Three Rivers where the rich and famous dwell. Not that we have anyone "famous" around here. Big houses on the Hill have expansive lawns maintained by local landscape services. Long, winding driveways lead to garages, with room for three, four, five, or more cars, where Caddies, Audis, and Jags are tucked in for the night.

When I was young, my mother drove us around this neighborhood at Christmastime to look at all the Christmas lights. I fantasized about living in one of these houses and always felt disappointed going home to our plain old house on our plain old street. Working-class houses for working-class folks.

Up here, in the rarefied environs of the West Hill, house-keepers, or at least maid services, bustle in and out during the week. Lush gardens are tended by gardeners. Children on the Hill don't have to mow lawns or pull weeds. Houses have pools—inground, maintained by pool people. It's rumored that more than one of these homes has an indoor pool. Such opulence boggles the mind.

On the West Hill, everything is fine. Bad things happen to *other* people. In the enclaves of the Hill, all is well. Everyone is safe. Safe from the big bad world. At least, that's what they'd like you to think.

But there are secrets on that hill. Dark, scary things that are hidden behind the facade of wealth and fake smiles.

My good friend Tansy Pemberley grew up at the tippy top of the West Hill. She became my first friend in middle school when our family moved to town. Tansy was rich, and I was not, but we hit it off. Tansy is the best friend anyone could have.

I was logging out of my computer, ready to go out investigating, when the front door of the office opened. A woman walked toward me with a blast of hot air—too hot for this early in the day—in her wake.

Black hair, big brown eyes, mid to late forties, I guessed. Broad shoulders. Great shape. Muscles. Tall and lean, she walked confidently, with machine-like precision. Her shiny black heels clicked across the tile. She wore a crisp white blouse, open to her cleavage, under a slate gray suit with a pencil skirt that accentuated her curvy lower half. The kind of suit my rich, big-city-investment-adviser sister Stephanie wears. The kind that would cost me a month's salary.

Rational Me was impressed. *Look at us, noticing all the details. Very detective-y!*

The woman marched to the counter, leaned in, and asked—no, demanded—"Who's in charge here?" Her voice had a husky undertone.

I stood up tall, pushed my shoulders back, chest out, chin up, trying to match her energy. I looked her in the eye, unsmiling. "I am."

She raised an eyebrow, skeptical, but she extended her hand. "Sheena Shay. Shay Investigations." Strong grip with her right hand as she produced a business card from her left jacket pocket.

I glanced at it. Big-city address. Big-city detective. Big deal. "What brings you to our little burg?"

She gave me a look. "I'd prefer to talk to whoever is *really* in charge."

I didn't want to go into the details of our operation, how Trip, Chief Bronson, and I are equal partners. "Then you should talk to me," I said.

Just then, Trip came in the back door. "I'm here, Mack!" he called as he headed to his office.

"Hey, Trip," I called. "We have a visitor."

Trip came to the reception area and looked at Sheena Shay. The term "gob-smacked" describes his reaction perfectly. Goofy-doofus and drooling-stupid also apply.

He extended a hand. "Trip Kipling."

When Sheena Shay extended her hand to him, a perfumed scent rose. Trip's nostrils flared, and he cleared his throat. His face twitched. I'm pretty sure his pupils dilated.

Snarky was disgusted. *Good grief. He's like a butterfly in heat.*

With her left hand, Sheena Shay snatched her business card from me and gave it to Trip. *The nerve.*

"Great to meet you," she said, husky voice smooth as silk. "Can we talk somewhere, uh"—she glanced at me, then back at him, lowered her voice, and added—"privately?"

"My office," he said. She followed him. She was just shy of six feet, exactly Trip's height. *Same height, same age. Perfect match. Yuck.*

After his office door closed, I said aloud to nobody, "What. The. Hell?" Snarky fumed. *The nerve! Just because he's a man? He must be the one in charge? Didn't that kind of thinking go out decades ago? How sexist. And she's a woman! Ridiculous!*

Badass Me added the B-word.

CHAPTER NINE

RIP AND THAT SHEENA person were in his office. I heard muf-
fled laughing and talking but couldn't hear what they said. I
put my head in my hands, trying to think.

A minute later, I heard the front door open. I looked up
as a young man—early twenties, maybe—came in. A mop of
light brown hair fluffed out over his forehead, strands sticking
to the sweat glistening there as he wrangled a briefcase and two
huge suitcases. He was tall and on the skinny side. Sweat rings
discolored the underarms of his short-sleeved, Western-style
shirt—popular with guys his age—in muted blue and green
plaid, with pearl snaps down the front. Jeans and sneakers completed the look.

He glanced around. "My boss came in here. Sheena Shay?"

"Oh yeah. She's talking with my partner." I pointed to Trip's
office.

He set the cases down. "I'm her assistant. Germany Jones."

"Mackenzie Prentice." We exchanged the "nice-to-meet-
yous," and I offered coffee. I headed to the kitchen, made a cup

of vanilla hazelnut for each of us, and grabbed creamers and sugar packets just in case.

When I came back, he'd settled into one of the reception area chairs and was paging through an old issue of *Guns and Ammo*.

"You can sit here by me if you'd like, Germany Jones."

He took the chair next to my desk, stirred three creams and two packets of sugar into his coffee.

"You have an interesting name, Germany Jones." I liked saying it.

He smiled as he pushed the hair off his forehead, wiping the sweat away with his palm. "I get that a lot. My dad was in the Air Force. I was born while he was stationed at Ramstein in Germany. My sister was born while he was stationed in the Far East."

"Let me guess. She's Japan Jones?"

He laughed. "Nope. My sister's name is Okinawa."

I liked Germany. He said he'd worked for Sheena Shay for two years. Sheena had worked for the police department in The City until she was fired. I perked up. "Fired? Geez, what'd she do?"

He took a sip of his coffee. "She threw a perp through a plate glass window when he resisted arrest. I guess she'd done other things before that, so that was the last straw."

After being fired, Sheena started her own investigations business, and Germany ran the office for her.

"So what brings you to Three Rivers? What's with the suitcases?"

He stared at the desk for a long moment. "We were moving to a new location anyway. Downtown rent was a little too steep, and Sheena was ready for a change." He paused, looked left and right, then continued, voice low. "The truth? There are some people in The City who, um, aren't real happy with Sheena right now. So she thought it would be a good idea for us to have a change of scene until things settle down."

"But why come here?"

"This old man in The City hired Sheena yesterday to look into a family matter for him. I don't have all the details, but Sheena said the timing was perfect. She just told me to pack up the office, and here we are."

Trip and Sheena emerged from his office. He whispered something to her, and she laid a hand on his arm while they laughed. Private joke. *Disgusting.*

They came to the counter in front of my desk. Trip said, "Mackenzie Prentice, meet Sheena Shay."

"We've met," I said. Cold. Pure ice.

Sheena smiled, a little gap between her front teeth. "I'm afraid I was rude before." Her voice was friendly enough, but there was something in her eyes. Challenge maybe? "Can we start over?"

I didn't want Trip to think I was the rude one, so I smiled and said, "Sure."

We shook again. Her grip was just short of painful. She said, "I look forward to working together."

Wait. What?

Trip said, "Mack, Sheena is here to investigate the Gordon case. We're all going to give her all the help she needs."

"Excuse me?" My throat got tight.

Sheena said, "The girl evidently went off some cliff around here. Her grandfather hired me. His daughter told him she'd hired your agency. He thought you could use my help. Evidently, his daughter—"

I held up a hand. "I'm familiar. Mrs. Gordon—that's Maisie's mother—came in yesterday and hired us—uh, *me*—to investigate. I've already started working the case."

Sheena said, "Well, it's a good thing I showed up, isn't it? Two heads—" She looked at Trip and batted her eyelashes. "*Three* heads are better than one."

Snarky's stomach turned. *Dis. Gus. TING!*

Trip gave a goofy grin. "Much better, yes. We can *all* benefit from your experience. Mack, Sheena worked as a cop in The City—"

I interrupted him. "I heard." I wonder if she'd told Trip the whole story.

Trip said, "Anyway, we'll all be working this case together. Clear?"

I waited a moment before I said, "Clear." *Whatever.*

Trip continued. "Oh, and Sheena will be setting up in the middle office."

My mouth went dry. Badass was furious. *The middle office? My office? The office that I'll be taking as soon as my license comes through and I'm an official investigator? What the—?*

Sheena looked at Germany. "You can get that office squared away, right, Germ?"

"Sure thing, Sheena."

Trip said, "Give him a hand, Mack. Get him set on the Wi-Fi. Show him the phone system, okay?"

I bit back what I really wanted to say. I nodded. "Sure. No problem." I gave Sheena a fake smile. She fake-smiled back. Oh, yeah, we were going to get along *very* well.

Trip said, over his shoulder as he and Sheena headed toward the back door, "I'm going to show Sheena around town. Not sure what time I'll be back."

"I'm not your secretary, Trip!" I hollered after him. I'm sure he didn't hear me since he and Sheena were whispering and giggling as they headed out to his BMW. *Ugh.*

After they left, I helped Germany move Sheena's things into the middle office. *My! Middle! Office!* Rational Me knew there was no need to take my anger and disappointment out on Germany. Snarky agreed. *Not his fault he works for such a pushy, manipulative, conniving, demanding—*

As we worked, I told Germany about our agency. How we got started. How I was temporarily managing the place while I waited for my license. "How about you, Germany? You do any investigating?"

"Nope," he said. "I keep things organized. I make coffee. Do paperwork. Make copies. Keep the books. Take calls. Set appointments."

"What kind of cases does she do?"

"She does a lot of spying on married people, trying to catch cheaters. Tracking down deadbeats. The usual stuff, right? I'm sure you know. Nothing too exciting."

"More exciting than missing parakeets." I told him about little Louisa's request that I find Banjo but assured him I'd done a lot more than that. How I'd tracked down a missing son, a kidnapped friend, and more than a couple of killers to date.

"Killers? Seriously? Dang!"

I filled him in on the details. Told him about my battles, my history with almost being shot, nearly being burned in my apartment and then in a cornfield, almost drowned in a urinal, choked, hit with a brick, and most recently, close to having my skull cracked with a hatchet.

"Whoa. Seriously? Impressive."

"Yeah, my cop-friend Heather Sullivan called me an 'impressive badass.'"

He said, "Sheena's tough, but it sounds like you're right there with her."

"Nah," I said, the soul of modesty. "Just doing my job, Germany. Just doing my job."

CHAPTER TEN

G ERMANY WAS GREAT. AND I admit it was nice to have someone admiring me. I invited him to come along as I started my investigation into Maisie's death.

"Seriously? I would love that!"

I figured maybe I could resolve this one before Sheena Shay even got started. Let her waste precious time canoodling—or whatever—with Trip. I was on the case.

I started my Ford Escape. I told Germany how I'd bought the car from my older brother Greg and it came with a cricket. "So I named the car Cricket."

The actual cricket took that moment to chirp from the back end of the car. "Germany, meet Jimbo. My traveling companion."

Germany laughed. He craned his neck to see the floor behind the driver's seat, where I'd provided a shallow bowl of Fluker's Cricket Quencher blue water gels and Orange Cube Complete cricket food I bought on Amazon. No sign of the cricket. "You feed it?"

"Yup. Least I can do," I said.

"How long do they live?"

I'd done my research and knew that Jimbo was well past his life expectancy. "He might stop chirping any time. Meanwhile, he's good company."

Germany directed his words toward the back. "Glad to meet you, Jimbo, wherever you are."

Jimbo said nothing.

As we drove, Germany peppered me with questions. *Nice kid. Smart kid.*

Our first stop was Tansy's yoga studio—River Bend Yoga—on River Street, not far from TriMak. She'd just finished teaching a class and was wiping her face with a towel. She'd pulled her long blonde hair into a topknot and wrapped a fluorescent green headband around it. The skin-tight top and leggings stretched over her tall, fit body were covered in green and orange iridescent swirls. I was pretty sure she'd glow in the dark.

"What's up, Mack?" She tossed the towel into a cloth hamper.

I introduced Germany, then asked, "You remember that girl, Maisie Gordon, who died on the cliff? Her mother wants me to investigate."

She frowned. "Investigate? That was a million years ago. And wasn't it suicide?"

"Twenty-two years, actually. It was the end of her sophomore year. Her mother doesn't believe she did it on purpose."

Tansy said, "How are you supposed to figure out if it wasn't suicide after all these years?"

"I don't know. But I'm going to start with talking to everyone who is still around." I read Tansy the list of names I'd jotted into my phone. Since the Gordons lived on the West Hill, maybe Maisie's friends did too. "Know any of these people?"

"Yes. Jemma Dalworthy. The Dalworthys lived near us. Jemma was older than me, more my brother's age."

"Maisie was fifteen, almost sixteen, when she died. Three years older than we were then."

"Sounds about right. The Dalworthys still live in the same house. The dad is a banker, and the mom is one of those social types. You know—the 'tennis and lunch at the country club' ladies."

I didn't know. My family is not *that* kind of family. We're definitely on the have-not side of society. Working class, middle class. Nothing country club about us. More likely to be cleaning the club and serving the lunch.

"Your mom isn't like that," I said. I always liked Mrs. Pemberley. When I went to Tansy's house for sleepovers, Mrs. P. made us root beer floats and had store-bought cookies and six different kinds of breakfast cereal in the morning. Luxury. "Your mom is great," I said.

Tansy smiled. "My mother has her causes—fundraising and that kind of thing, but she's very down-to-earth. Always has been. She didn't grow up with money."

"You knew the Dalworthys," I said, getting back on the investigatory track.

Tansy nodded. "Yeah. And I remember there was something about something back in the day. Something about the dad and his bank, maybe? I don't know exactly."

"What about this other friend—Onyx Lyden? Is she a West Hill girl too?"

"Yes. I remember her. They lived down the hill."

The richest families lived highest "up the hill." People like the Pemberleys, Judge Rollo Carson and his family, and Trip's family. The movers and shakers of Three Rivers, living the high life on the highest hill. The upper crust.

The pecking order of those less "crusty" was indicated by their location farther "down the hill." Middle-hilllers had higher status than lower-hillers.

But the least of these hill-dwellers were still higher in social standing than the rest of us—living as flatlanders in the rest of Three Rivers. And, of course, we in the flatlands still had higher social status than the poor folks living in the Bottoms along the river.

Amazing how we humans divide ourselves.

"Remember anything about Onyx? Her family?"

Tansy thought a moment. "Not really. I didn't know her back then, but she came to one of my yoga classes a couple years ago. I think she's a nurse at the hospital."

That confirmed what Yolanda had told me at the gym. "Remember anything else?"

Tansy took a beat. "Yeah. I remember that Maisie's older sister Charity was super protective of her. You never saw Maisie outside without her sister Charity. Joined at the hip."

"Did you go to her funeral, Tans?"

"Yes, our whole family went. I remember her mother just sitting there, not crying. She just looked kind of frozen. Her sister didn't cry either. Just stood by the casket forever, staring at her sister. Not a tear. Weird. If it was my brother's funeral, I'd have been bawling my eyes out."

We fell silent a moment. I was trying not to imagine a funeral for anyone I loved.

I asked, "Is there anything else you can tell me about the Gordons?"

Tansy thought for a second, then said, "I think the mom got a lot of money when her husband died. That's probably how she could afford to stay on the Hill. I think I heard she was real depressed, like never leaving the house. I can ask my mom if she knows anything more. Would that help?"

"Can't hurt to ask." I told Tansy I'd see her later, and Germany and I headed toward our next stop.

CHAPTER ELEVEN

G ERMANY SAID HE DIDN'T mind waiting in the car while I went into Three Rivers PD to talk with Heather. I'd texted her on the way, and she okayed me to stop by.

Heather Sullivan is my primary contact with the police. We get along unless she gets mad at me for "messing around in police business." Which I do on occasion. But not intentionally. I'm just trying to get answers for people. She shouldn't get mad at me for that.

And I figured she certainly couldn't get mad at me for checking into this case since it all went down over twenty years ago.

I left Germany playing on his phone in the car, the engine and the AC running. Heather might tolerate me, but she might not tolerate having another civilian snooping with me.

The officer on duty at the front desk buzzed Heather's office. "She'll see you. You know where her office is?"

I nodded. He opened the partition, and I headed down the hall. Heather was on the phone. She held up an index finger, and I waited at the open door until she waved me in.

"What's up, Mack?" She was in a jovial mood. Good start.

"I'm on a new case."

"Hey, you got your license? Congrats!" She smiled.

"Not quite yet. I did the test online. Just waiting for the state licensing department to do their thing."

"So you're not official then. You're doing something for a family member or a friend?"

"I'm acting under the chief's authority. He gave me the okay to do the background investigation with this case."

Since Chief Bronson had been Heather's boss until last year, she must have decided it was okay for me to be working on the case.

"Okay, so what have you got?" she asked. "How can I help?"

Very friendly mood. "It's the Maisie Gordon case. She went off the 3R cliff twenty-some years ago. Everyone said it was a suicide."

Heather said, "And you're digging into it? Why?"

I explained about Maisie's mother and the cancer and the urgency and the sympathy I felt.

"Nice of you to care, Mackenzie, but I don't know how you're going to change the facts."

"But we don't know for sure what the facts are."

"Well, we're ninety-nine point nine percent sure."

"How do you even know that? Have you *checked* the facts? You're just assuming that everyone back then did their job and nothing got ignored."

She sat up straighter. "Hey, don't go insulting the people who serve and protect."

"No disrespect intended, but isn't it possible that somebody could have missed something back then? Not as sophisticated then as now, right? Somebody might have assumed that just because she left a note, it was suicide."

She frowned. "She left a note. Who would leave a note if it wasn't suicide?"

"The note was vague. 'It's all too much,' it said. That could mean anything. Too much homework. Too much worry. Too much—"

Heather jumped in. "Or 'too much for me to handle, so I'm going to jump off the cliff.'"

"But she didn't say that."

Heather raised her voice. "She didn't *not* say it either. Sometimes things are just what they seem to be. You're probably wasting your time. And mine."

"Ugh!" I said and crossed my arms. "You just don't get it."

She took a breath, softened her tone. "I think I do, Mack. You want to help. It's how you are. You want this woman to have closure—well, you hope you can give her the closure she *wants* instead of the closure she already *has*. You're going to do what you're going to do. Just don't be dissing my predecessors or this department."

"I have a couple questions for you."

She looked at her watch. "And I have a meeting in one minute, so make it quick."

"I've requested a copy of the investigation."

"Yep, that would be public record. You don't need me for that."

"Well, when I get the copies, if I have questions, can I ask you?"

"If I have the time, sure." She stood. "I really have to get to my meeting. C'mon. I'll walk you out."

We headed toward the front door. Heather asked, "How's your grandmother doing? Haven't seen her in here lately." She winked at me.

My grandmother and her friend Velma had gotten involved with a case of mine despite my warning them not to. "Gram didn't like, as she put it, 'getting hauled in for questioning.' I warned her to stop butting in, and she's sworn off snooping."

"So sticking your nose in where it doesn't belong is a family trait. Irritating, isn't it, when someone gets involved in your business?" Heather said with a smile as she headed outside.

I wrinkled my nose at her. I know a passive-aggressive comment when I hear one.

CHAPTER TWELVE

IT WAS ALMOST ONE-THIRTY. I offered to drop Germany back at TriMak so he could finish organizing for Sheena. He gave me puppy-dog eyes. "Can't I please hang with you? Sheena never takes me along on cases."

I felt sorry for him, stuck in the office all the time. It was lunchtime, so we swung into Java Java on the way back to the office and got two hot turkey hoagies to go, chips, and a couple diet Cokes.

Back at the car, I tore a piece of lettuce off my sandwich and dropped it into Jimbo's food dish before I got into the driver's seat.

"Where to next?" Germany asked.

"I want to go up to the cliff, check it out. Maybe I'll see something new." I'd been to the cliff plenty of times growing up in Three Rivers, but I wanted a fresh look from the perspective of the investigation.

"Cool! Let's go!" Germany was an enthusiastic sidekick, to say the least.

I headed Cricket toward the Woodson Avenue bridge. I pointed across the river to the cliff face rising a hundred feet or so above the rocks on the river's shore. "That's where we're headed. See that bluff up there?"

Germany scrunched forward and looked up. "What's that carved on it? Looks like a three?"

"It's a number three and a capital letter R," I explained. "For Three Rivers."

"Oh, duh. Of course," Germany said. "Who put it there? That took guts."

"Don't know. It was years ago, but it's kind of a big deal around here. Like a landmark."

We were halfway across the bridge when my cell buzzed. Lou Burgess. She owns Lou's Vintage on River Street. I'd held a very part-time job helping Lou organize her vintage shop since the previous fall. Lou helped me out when I needed a job. I help her out when she needs it now. A mutually satisfying arrangement.

I tapped my earbud to answer. (Hands-free is the only safe way to go, my anxious mother warns me. Often.)

Lou said, "Mackenzie, I have something here you just have to see. Can you swing by today? I could use some advice."

Cat, meet curiosity.

I figured the cliff would still be there later. I did a U-turn and headed back the way we'd come, explaining the Lou situation to Germany as I drove.

Lou was in her back room when we arrived. In her seventies, Lou describes herself as "an old hippie." True to form, she had on bell-bottom jeans and a blue tee shirt emblazoned with a yellow peace sign. Her long gray hair hung down her back in a braid, intertwined with several strands of blue and yellow yarn.

She'd attached sparkly beads at the ends of the yarn. The beads clicked together softly as she moved.

After introductions, Lou said, "I bid on a storage unit. You know, like on that *Storage Wars* TV show? An old woman died, and her son sold off the big stuff in the house. Then he just put whatever was left in the storage unit. He stopped paying on it, and the manager auctioned it off. I won." She seemed particularly pleased with herself. "You never know what you're going to get with something like that, but I took a chance." She gestured toward the front of the shop. "Got some great stuff. Let me show you."

Germany and I followed her to a mannequin sporting a silky black dress. "This is iconic. It's like the original 'little black dress.' Check it out." She showed us the label.

I gave a slow whistle. "Wow. A Dior. What's it worth, Lou?"

She showed me the price tag she'd hung on it. I whistled again. "Eight hundred dollars, Lou? Seriously? For a dress?"

She grinned. "For a vintage Dior? That's a bargain, trust me. Just look at it." Her voice had a reverent tone. "It's perfect. That cinched waist. The full skirt. Classic Dior."

"Well, congrats, Lou. I've got to get back to work now."

She grabbed my arm. "Wait. The dress isn't why I called you." She led me back to the storeroom. She picked up a red velvet cloth bag and handed it to me. "Take a look."

I opened the drawstring and looked inside. My throat caught. "Is this what I think it is?" I held it toward Germany. He made a face.

I set the bag on top of a cardboard box and pulled out the contents.

An urn.

"Holy crap," Germany whispered. "What's in it?"

"You mean, *who's* in it," I said.

"Who indeed," Lou said.

I shivered. "Is it the old woman? Would her son have left her like that?"

"Or maybe it's her husband."

Germany asked, "Have you looked inside?"

Lou shook her head. "Seems sacrilegious to do that. Like disturbing a grave."

Germany's turn to shiver.

I said, "Lou, she—or whoever—is in a sack. Abandoned in a storage unit. Already disturbed, I'd say. I'm going to look." I had a morbid curiosity about looking into the urn. What do they call it? Cremains?

I unscrewed the lid, peeked in. "Looks like ashes." My stomach tightened. Lou was right. Sacrilege. Violating someone's privacy. I screwed the lid back on.

I said, "Maybe we should contact her son? See what he wants to do with it?"

Lou shook her head. "He's nowhere to be found, the storage unit manager said. That's why the unit was sold off."

My newbie investigator mind started working. "Where was the unit? Maybe I can track the guy down." Lou gave me the details, and I made notes in my phone.

She said, "Are you sure you want to do this? It's probably a waste of time."

"Good practice for me. I'll see what I can find out."

"Well, don't stress about it. If you find the guy, great. If not, it's okay."

I said, "If we find out this is the old woman and can't find the son, what do we do with her ashes?"

Lou shrugged. "I'm not sure. I guess we could scatter them somewhere nice. Not really up to me to bury her or anything. But I don't want her hanging around the store either."

Lou's turn to shiver.

I told Lou I'd let her know what I found out, and Germany and I headed back toward the cliff.

CHAPTER THIRTEEN

LEFT CRICKET IN THE parking lot at Cliffside Park. Germany and I started the climb to the top of the 3R cliff. Short, steep sections of stairs made from old railroad ties are embedded into the hill, with a wooden railing on each side. Then there are spans of sandy, rocky path, where the incline isn't as steep. More stairs. More path. Onward and upward.

All along the trail, I recognized patches of Queen Anne's lace, with its hairy stems and basket-like structures that open into clusters of little white flowers. I also noticed huge growths of buckthorn, an invasive species that Gram has declared war on in her yard. I've spent hours with her trying to uproot what she calls "the devil bush."

And interspersed among the flowers and the buckthorn, swaths of wild blackberries—thick, prickly, and unassailable.

Fifteen minutes of huffing and puffing later, Germany and I reached the top, stepping around the last of the thorny blackberry brambles onto the clifftop—thirty feet or so of sandy soil and rocks with a knee-high guard rail a yard or so from the edge.

When I was a child, there was no guardrail. My grandfather warned us children, "You need to use the sense God gave you and stay back from the edge. If people get too close and fall, that's on them."

The chief feels the same way. He says, "We can't police everything. It's about personal responsibility. It's like the person who sues a restaurant because they spill hot coffee on themselves. What do you expect when you order hot coffee? You can't hang on to it, that's your problem."

Following that line of thinking, *Maisie, what did you expect would happen when you stepped to the edge of the cliff?*

Germany and I stood side by side, looking out over the river. Windswept is a good word to describe the top of the 3R cliff. Wind swirls up from the river far below and whirls around the clifftop, at times so strong that it's hard to keep your balance.

Today was such a time. The wind blasted us, whipping my hair into my face. It caught Germany's mop of hair and blew it straight up, then sideways. The next gust carried sand up from the ground. I shut my eyes for a moment and felt a wave of vertigo.

Did the wind do this to you, Maisie? Maybe she ventured too close to the edge, got dizzy, and the wind swept her over. That was a possibility.

Except there was that note.

"What do you think happened?" Germany asked.

I looked at him. "Maybe the girl just had a dramatic moment where she stood at the cliff's edge, mourning an unrequited love. Her mother said she might have had a crush on some boy whose name starts with B, but no idea who the boy was."

"How can they be sure it was a boy?" Germany asked.

"Hmm. Never thought of that. Good point." That opened a whole new passel of possibilities. "Maybe she decided her life wasn't worth living, fifteen-year-old drama style. 'He'll be sorry, or they'll be sorry when I'm gone. I'll show them.' That kind of thinking. Maybe every teenager has those moments. You know, when we can't get what we want. When we feel we don't fit in. When we've been rejected."

Germany nodded. "I get that. Sometimes the pressure for grades, the peer pressure, is too much."

"That's what her note said. 'It's all too much.'"

We stood together, looking into the distance. Maybe a romance with this B person, whoever it was, had gone sour. I told Germany, "I dated my ex in high school, and we certainly had fights. High teenaged drama. Did I ever want to end my life? No. It was never that bad for me."

"Same here," he said.

"You never thought about killing yourself?"

He shrugged. "Maybe everybody thinks about it. But it was never that bad. Once I got kind of depressed, and my parents threatened to make me go to therapy. That snapped me out of it." He chuckled.

I laughed. "My grandmother says, 'We couldn't afford therapy, so we just coped.'"

I pointed across the river. "That gray roof is our office. And over there is Donatello's. Best Italian food around."

"I love Italian," he said.

"And that red roof over there is Tansy's yoga studio."

Germany smiled. "She was cool. Is she single?"

I smiled. "Tansy is my age, Germany. Way too old for you."

His cheeks reddened. "Doesn't hurt to ask." He got quiet.

A hot gust of wind brought more dust. Germany covered his eyes with his arm. I averted my face and sneezed.

From the west, a tall cloud bank approached. Meteorologist Stuart Klump had predicted a thunderstorm later in the day.

I wondered what the weather had been like the night of Maisie's death. Had there been a storm? Or was it a clear night and the last thing she saw was the starry sky? I needed to do some research. Maybe the weather was a factor. Maybe it was wet and slippery up here. Slippery footing might spell accidental death.

I came back to the moment in time to see Germany step over the guard rail and walk toward the edge.

My stomach dropped. "Germany! Not too close!"

He shot me a look. "Okay, Mom."

Geez, he's an adult. Not your child. I had a sudden sympathy for Gram and my mother and all the worrying they did over the health and safety of their children and grandchildren.

"Sorry!" I said. I'm not a fan of heights, but I steeled myself and stepped over the rail. Three feet of sandy soil between me and oblivion.

Germany peered over the edge. "Those rocks down there are wicked."

I craned my neck to peek. My stomach lurched. My heart thumped. Huge boulders lined the shore of the river, a hundred feet or so below, with a narrow strip of sand to the water's edge. Wicked, indeed.

I pictured Maisie standing here. A skinny, little fifteen-year-old—"not much to her," Gram would say. I imagined her, with that "all too much" feeling, contemplating life and death.

A strong wind could have caught her and taken her off balance.

Thunder rumbled. The clouds to the west were darker, split by near-constant lightning. A sudden gust of chilly wind hit me. The day had been hot and humid, and now a cold front had arrived. I crossed my arms and rubbed my triceps.

Germany asked, "What are we looking for up here?"

"I just wanted to get a feel for the scene. What it might have been like for Maisie Gordon."

He looked over the edge again. "Nasty fall for her, I'd say. Those rocks look hard."

"Understatement."

Waves of thunder came from the distance. The clouds roiled, darker and denser. More lightning in the west. "We'd better get down from here." I stepped back over the rail.

Germany stayed put, his arms spread wide at the cliff's edge, head thrown back. The wind grabbed at his shirt, blew his hair back.

I jumped at a huge crash of thunder. "Germany! What the heck are you doing?"

"Feelin' it! I'm just feelin' it!" He shouted above the wind. "Feel the power! God, I love storms!"

I thought about Nathan's "fool brother" standing before the tornado. Did Maisie Gordon love storms too?

I reached over the guard rail and tugged on the back of his shirt. "Come on! You really don't want to be the tallest thing around when there's lightning."

Germany turned around, hung his head, shoved his lower lip out, and dug the toe of one sneaker into the sandy soil. "Aw, Mom, you're spoiling all my fun!"

"Don't be an idiot," I said and gave him a playful slap on the shoulder.

He laughed and climbed over the rail.

As we drove back to TriMak, I reviewed the facts aloud. "Fifteen-year-old Maisie Gordon went off the cliff and died. She left a note—short and cryptic, which may or may not have been a suicide note. Her mother is dying and wants to know for sure what happened to Maisie. She needs closure. Maisie's grandfather hired Sheena to come here for the same reason—closure."

Germany asked, "Do you think you're wasting your time?"

"I don't know. But I do know that Mrs. Gordon needs to know what happened, and I'm going to do my best to give her an answer."

"What if she doesn't like the answer?"

"That's how this works, Germany. People want us to find the truth but don't always like what we find."

CHAPTER FOURTEEN

RIVING BACK TO TRIMAK, I got an email from the police department saying the death investigation report was ready for pickup. Germany stayed in the car again, playing games on his phone while I ran inside.

Heather was at the front desk when I got there and handed me the report. "Come on back to my office. I pulled the photos for you."

An act of unprecedented generosity on her part.

She pointed to the chair in front of her desk. "Bring that around here."

She ordered. I obeyed.

She opened the nine-by-twelve envelope on her desk. "These are not for public consumption. Too upsetting for the families—for average people—to see."

"Understandable," I said. It's hard enough to see a stranger's dead body. I can't imagine seeing someone I loved like that. I swallowed hard as she took out a stack of a couple dozen eight-by-ten color photos.

Crime scene photos. Maisie's death scene. I sucked in my breath. This felt sacred somehow. Like I was invited into a privileged space, a private space. A space for the dead, not the living.

The first pictures were taken at the base of the cliff. Body-free pictures of the general area. The boulders, the shoreline of the Wolf River. Establishing the general feel of the place, I assumed. Time stamps indicated they were taken around five-thirty a.m. on June 13th. Just a few weeks before Maisie's sixteenth birthday. *Poor kid.*

Near one boulder, a yellow marker with a number three on it next to a pink-and-yellow flip-flop.

Then there was Maisie Gordon. Face down, her body sprawled awkwardly across several large rocks, her head at an odd ankle to her neck. Blood splattered across the rocks. More photos from different angles. Her head, her legs, her arms. Her one bare foot. The pink-and-yellow flip-flop dangling from the other. Heather flipped from shot to shot.

I noticed something. "Wait. Go back."

"What?" She returned to the previous photo.

I pointed. "Why is her right arm out of her hoodie?"

Heather shrugged. "Who knows? Maybe she was trying to take it off."

"Why would she do that when she was ready to jump off the cliff?"

"No idea. Maybe it just came off during the fall."

"Or maybe someone was fighting with her and grabbed it."

Heather said, "Or maybe they were trying to save her."

Maybe. Maybe. Maybe. Too many questions. Not enough answers. I leaned back in my chair. "Heather, why are you helping me with this?"

She said, "I thought about the mother—Mrs. Gordon. It's nice of you to try to get the answers she needs." She frowned. "But don't think this means I'll be letting you help me with real crime-solving in the future."

"Aw shucks. I thought maybe we were going to be BFFs now."

She shook her head. "Mackenzie, you know that the line between your work and mine is very clearly drawn. Don't mess around in cop business. Stay away from our active cases. And don't mess with crime scenes. Understand?"

"But you've been happy to have my help in the past when you were stuck. It's a one-way street then, isn't it? How fair is that?"

"I've told you before. I appreciated your help, but I can't reciprocate. It's just the way things are."

"Fine. I scratch your back, and you stab me in mine."

She scoffed. "Oh, please. Spare me the drama."

"Getting back to how you think I'm nice?"

"Yes, it's nice of you to want to help Mrs. Gordon. And just to prove I'm not the heartless rule-follower you think I am, I'll do what I can to help. Within the bounds of the law, of course. And within the restrictions of our various capacities."

"Lots of words there, Detective. Are you saying you'll help?"

"If I can, yes."

"Can I have copies of the photos?"

She shook her head. "Nope. I already told you they're not for public consumption. But I'll keep them for you, right here in my file cabinet for the time being."

I stood and thanked her. I left smiling.

Nice to have Heather's help, however limited it might be.

CHAPTER FIFTEEN

T RIP'S BLUE BMW WAS there when Germany and I pulled
onto the concrete parking pad behind TriMak. We made it
inside just as the rain started.

Sheena poked her head out of the middle office and yelled
at Germany, "Where the hell have you been?"

He looked at me and rolled his eyes. He followed Sheena
back into the office as she harped. "We've got a million things
to do, and you go off—"

"Stop," Germany said, his voice firm, even. "We'll get things
squared away here. Just calm down."

I heard Sheena give a loud exhale as Germany shut the
office door. *Look how he handles the witch. Masterful.*

I headed to the front of the office, took the urn out of the
bag, and set it on my desk. I examined it more closely. No
engraved initials. No name. No RIP MOTHER. No identifying
marks of any kind. *Okay, whoever you are. You can hang out here
until we figure out what to do with you.*

The chief came from his office, dressed in old man makeup. Bushy gray brows, with a couple of fake moles stuck on his face above a drooping gray handlebar mustache. A gray wig completed the look. The chief likes to work undercover, digging into old cases from his time with the police department. Cases with what he calls "unsatisfactory resolutions."

"Hey, Chickie, have you seen my cane? I had it here the other day." The cane is another costume prop.

I glanced around my desk. "Nope, sorry. Haven't seen it."

He patted the urn. "New client?" He chuckled at his own joke.

I explained Lou's situation.

"Uh, Chickie, identifying dead bodies isn't exactly in our job description."

"But I'd like to help Lou if I can. What would you do, Chief?"

"What do *you* think you should do, Chickie?" The chief is determined to make an investigator out of me.

"I guess I'd start with the storage unit," I said.

"That's what I'd do," he said over his shoulder as he headed back to his office.

Using the information Lou had given me, I made a quick phone call to the manager of the storage unit in Stone Creek, a lovely little town just northwest of Three Rivers. In a small town like that, everybody knows everything about everybody. The manager—a woman named Sharon—filled me in.

Bernard Weatherby rented the unit after his mother died. He'd auctioned off whatever he could sell from his mother's home and rented the unit for the rest. He told Sharon he'd be back to clear it all out, but he never returned. He quit paying for the unit, and after the legally allowed time, Sharon sold it off.

I thanked her and ended the call. Online, I found an obituary for Marion Weatherby posted on the *Stone Creek Courier* website. Just shy of one hundred when she died, Marion passed away peacefully at her home in Stone Creek.

She was one of seven children and the last to go. Preceded in death by her husband, Lawrence Weatherby. Survived by her son, Bernard, of Los Angeles. Only child. No mention of a spouse or children for Bernard.

I wondered if Marion had been ill, and, if so, who had cared for her in her last days. She'd passed away at home. Had she had dementia? Did her son care for her? Was he a kind and patient caregiver, like Gram was for Nathan? I hoped so.

There had been a private interment service at Stone Creek Cemetery. Marion was probably buried next to her husband.

I walked back to the chief's office with my laptop. He'd dressed in his shabby old man clothes. I'd seen this costume before. "Listen to this, Chief." I read him the obituary.

He frowned. "If the woman was buried, who is in the urn?"

"Good question," I said, Spidey senses tingling. "Ooh, what if it's a murder victim?"

He frowned again. "Think about it, Chickie. If you killed somebody, would you have them cremated?"

"I would if I was an undertaker," I said.

The chief's furry brows went up as he gave a slight smile. I read that as approval. Admiration even. Begrudging, maybe, but admiration, nevertheless.

The chief nodded. "Huh. I'll make a few calls. Check for unsolveds or missing persons in the Stone Creek area in the last few years. I'll let you know."

Nice to be connected to somebody with connections.

Later, as I packed up to leave for the day, the chief filled me in. According to the police and sheriff's departments in the Stone Creek area, there were no unsolved murders, no missing persons. Nothing.

I called Lou to let her know the person in the urn was a mystery.

She said, "Whoever it is, I think they need to go back to Stone Creek."

CHAPTER SIXTEEN

IT WAS ALMOST FIVE o'clock Wednesday night when I got home. Nobody else was there. No sign of dinner cooking. Odd. I hoped everything was okay.

Rational Me offered reassurance. *Listen to you, worrying about everybody. Gram is fine. Nathan's fine. Your mother is fine. Stop being anxious.*

Easy to say. Hard to do.

I sat at the dining room table and slid the police paperwork from the envelope. My stomach tightened at the heading: DEATH INVESTIGATION REPORT.

Not just some random report. *Maisie Gordon's* death investigation. A girl with a mother and a sister and a grandfather. A young girl with dreams, with hopes, with a future cut short.

I swallowed hard and read on. *Focus on the facts, just the facts.*

DECEASED: Maisie Gordon. DOB: Fourth of July, like her mother had said. AGE: 15.

DECEASED FOUND BY: William Fenning.

RELATIONSHIP: Passerby. Mrs. Gordon had mentioned that an early morning hiker had found the body. Date and time indicated Maisie had been there all night.

Poor girl. Alone all night in the dark and cold. I shivered. *Back to the facts.*

DECEASED LAST SEEN BY: Jemma Dalworthy (friend) at 10:15 p.m. the night she died. Interesting.

I read on. Maisie's description. So clinical. So impersonal. Under CONDITION OF BODY were the gruesome details. Consistent with the photos I'd seen. Dirty. Bloody. Fixed lividity. Complete rigor. She'd lain there a long time before the hiker spotted her.

More details were on the second page of the report. Maisie was declared dead on the scene. NEXT OF KIN: Felicity Gordon, mother.

FIRST OFFICER ON SCENE: Wade Clark. A quick online search brought up his obituary. He'd been dead five years.

PRIMARY CASE OFFICER: Harlan Burling. Still living in Three Rivers, according to Google. The form indicated he was the one who notified Maisie's mother of her death.

The form asked, "Was this death related to domestic violence?" The box for NO was checked. That was the assumption.

The section describing the scene seemed consistent with what the photos had shown me. Rocks. Body. One flip-flop on, one off. "Partially clothed" likely referred to her arm being out of the sweatshirt. The report indicated her underclothing was in place. *Thank goodness.*

SUSPECTED MANNER OF DEATH: I read the list. So many ways for a person to go. Shooting, cutting, burning, poisoning. Stabbing, crushing, hanging, drowning.

Blunt force trauma. That was checked for Maisie. A human skull hitting those rocks from that height? Trauma, indeed.

SUSPECTED CAUSE OF DEATH: Suicide. And near that, someone had written: "See attached." I flipped to the last page, after the hand drawing of the scene and the drawings of human figures indicating her injuries.

A photocopy of the note in a young girl's handwriting. "It's all too much." Just like her mother said.

End of the form. End of the story.

I slid the paperwork back into the envelope and sat with my eyes closed. *This is how we end*, I thought. *All our days—our lifetime—of living and loving end like this. A piece of paper—the final piece—with the cold, hard facts. A death certificate. An obituary summarizing an entire life in a few short paragraphs.*

A heavy cloud of sadness settled over me. I wanted a glass of wine. Wine helps everything, especially sadness.

Gram and Nathan came in the back door. "We brought KFC," Gram said, as the smell of finger-lickin' goodness filled the room.

"Too hot to cook," Gram said.

Fortunately, I wasn't too sad to eat.

CHAPTER SEVENTEEN

T HUNDER BOOMED AS GRAM and I cleaned up after dinner. I
washed. She dried. Rain pelted the window above the sink.
"This rain is a relief," Gram said.

"It's been so muggy. Miserable," I said.

She nodded. "And this old house, with no central air."

"At least the window units keep the bedrooms cool," I said.
"You know they make these units that you mount on the wall
now, Gram. Nick said he'd be glad to get some for you. You can
cool the whole house with those if you want. Or just cool the
room you're in."

"Oh, I've lived this long without it. I think I can manage,"
she said. "It pays to have *sisu*." Ah, yes, that mysterious quality
of strength and resilience Gram has, inherited from her Finnish
forebears. She tells me I have it too.

I said, "I don't have enough sisu to help me when the
weather is this miserable."

"Ha! This is nothing," Gram said and chatted on about her
childhood on the farm. Her parents and siblings coping with

the heat of the midwestern summers, the hordes of biting flies, and the clouds of mosquitoes. Sleeping outside or under wet sheets. In the winter, huddling under quilts in their attic bedroom as snow drifted in through cracks in the walls.

Listening to her tales, I feel like a total wuss. "Nick put a central air unit in the carriage house, so if it gets too bad in here, you can always move in with me," I said.

"Thanks, dear, but I think we'll be okay." She hung her dishtowel to dry.

As I drained the dishwater from the sink, my mother came in the back door, eyes red and puffy. Mascara rivers streaked her cheeks.

"You look awful, dear," Gram said.

My mother scowled. "Gee, thanks, Ma!"

"What's the matter?" I said.

"It's that jerk, Duncan!" She spat the words. "*He's* what's the matter!"

Duncan was a great guy, and dating him had been good for my mother, drawing her out of her shell, calming her anxiety.

She headed past me toward the dining room. I intercepted her, put an arm around her. "Mom, sit down. Tell us what's going on."

She sat, reluctantly, in one of the wooden chairs at the kitchen table. Shoulders slumped, she let out a sigh. "Duncan is a jerk! I don't know what I ever saw in him."

We waited.

"I caught him texting with another woman." She hung her head and moaned. "I should have known better." She looked at us. "It's like I've always said. There are only two kinds of men in the world—those who have already let us down and those who are going to!" My mother had been adamantly single for years until she connected with Duncan. She let out a sob, leaned her elbows on the table, and put her face in her hands.

"Who is she?" I asked.

"Someone he used to work with," she said into her palms.

Gram asked, "At the shoe factory? That's where *you* met Duncan. Do you know this woman?"

My mother raised her head and glared at Gram. "I *know* that's where I met him. And *no*, I don't *know* this woman."

I clenched my teeth. The storm outside wasn't the only one.

My mom blew out a sigh. "We're supposed to be"—another sigh—"exclusive." She bit back a sob. "At least I *thought* we were." She crossed her arms on the table and laid her head down.

Gram looked at me. I shrugged.

Gram said, her voice gentle. "So, Barbara, they texted. Everybody texts everybody these days. So what?"

My mother glared harder. "*So what*? Don't you know what this *means*? He's texting other women. Who knows if she's the only one. And they are friends on Facebook too."

I said, "That's not really proof of any wrongdoing, is it?"

My turn for the glare. "Oooh! Well, aren't you just Miss Big-Time Detective now!"

I knew my mother was deflecting her anger for Duncan, and I was simply in the line of fire. I wasn't going to take it personally. "No need to get snippy, Mom. I'm on your side."

"Well, it doesn't sound like it. It sounds like you're defending the big jerk."

Everything had been going so well with my mother and Duncan. I'd gotten used to the fact that they were a couple. I wasn't even jealous anymore, especially since I had a guy of my own. Sort of. And maybe even two guys. Kind of.

Gram said, "What proof do you have that he's actually cheating on you, Barbara? I mean when Chester cheated on me, everyone at the senior center knew about it." Gram's second husband, the late Chester, had died in the senior center parking lot, in a compromising position with a woman we all call "The Hussy." Publicly embarrassing for all parties involved.

I pressed. "Have you actually *seen* Duncan doing anything? Any proof?"

She snarled. "I saw the text. And he likes everything on her Facebook page. Isn't that enough?"

I considered. "So, he sent her a text. What did it say?"

"'Happy birthday. You look great.' If that's not suggestive of something else, I don't know what is!"

I asked, "What did Duncan say when you asked him about it?"

"Humph! I'm not going to ask him! I don't want him to think I was snooping around."

"But you were."

"Well, he doesn't have to know that. I told him it's over. I told him things just aren't going to work between us. I'm cutting my losses and moving on." She started crying harder, and the last words came out in a loud lament. "I . . . should have . . . known better!"

Ah, my mother still carried the old wounds. She'd vowed to never get involved with another man, and now here she was, in love with Duncan and afraid of another broken heart.

Gram said, "Barbara, don't you think you should at least hear what the man has to say?"

I added, "Duncan loves you. That's obvious. And we all love him. Are you going to blow up the relationship, maybe for no reason?"

My mother swiped her palms across her cheeks and glowered at us both. "It's reason enough for me! I'm going to bed!" With that, she got up and stormed out of the kitchen.

"Well, don't that beat all?" Gram said.

"Shocker, that's for sure," I said.

Gram let out a sigh. "I thought those two would make it to 'happily ever after.' Dang it. What's wrong with men?"

"I don't know, Gram. But she just might be overreacting."

Gram nodded in agreement. "Not the first time she's done that."

My mother's anxiety had carried her away for as long as I could remember. She took up running ten years ago, she said, to burn off her anxious energy. Running hasn't helped her much. She's still the harbinger of worst-case scenarios, the bearer of worst possible news. A glass-completely-empty kind of person.

Duncan had cheered her up and made her a little more optimistic. I was sorry to think that might be coming to an end.

Gram said, "Maybe it's just this heat. It's got us all on edge. Maybe I should talk to Duncan. Get his side of the story. I'm sure there's an innocent explanation. What do you think?"

I said, "Might be worth a try."

"Will you do it with me?"

I hesitated. Would I want my mother talking to any guy in my life? Absolutely not. My mother's angst would probably scare anyone away. That old idea of "look at the mother when you date the daughter" thing.

But this was Gram. Sweet, gentle, caring Gram. What harm would it do? "Okay," I said, "I'll talk to Duncan with you."

I hoped I wouldn't regret saying that.

CHAPTER EIGHTEEN

AFTER MY MOTHER HEADED upstairs to bed, Gram scooped maple nut ice cream into three bowls. She delivered one to Nathan, who was in the family room watching a rerun of *The Andy Griffith Show* on the family-friendly TV channel.

She set the other two bowls on the dining room table and said, "Come. Sit. I have something to tell you."

As I sat, my stomach knotted. "Sounds serious. Is something wrong, Gram?"

She patted my arm and smiled. "Heavens no, sweetie! I just heard something I thought you should know." Gram meets with her friends at Hilda's Café every Monday morning to catch up on the latest news about who is doing what with whom in Three Rivers. I shouldn't be surprised anymore by how much Gram knows about things—even things that should be confidential. Three Rivers is a small place, and its grapevine is huge.

"What is it, Gram?"

She leaned in, mischief in her little blue eyes. "It's about the Gordon case."

I frowned at her. "What do you mean? The Gordon case, if there even *is* a 'Gordon case'"—I air quoted—"would be *TriMak* business, not *yours*." Heather was right. It *is* annoying when people stick their noses in your business. "You have to leave the investigating to me."

"It's not like I'm *doing* anything. I just heard something and thought you'd be interested. But if you're not—" She shoveled a big chunk of maple nut into her mouth and looked away.

"Okay, okay, I'm sorry. What is it you heard?"

She swallowed and smiled. "Well . . ." She paused for effect. "Velma's brother's wife's sister—"

"Hold on. Who is your friend Velma's brother's wife's sister?"

"The one I'm talking about. Just listen!"

I sat back, crossed my arms. "I'm listening."

"Velma's brother's wife's sister is Greta Bullfinch." Gram looked at me as if I should know this person. I did not.

"And this Bullfinch person is . . . ?"

She let out an exasperated breath. "She was the Carsons' housekeeper."

"So your friend's relative was a housekeeper."

"Yes, for the *Carsons*." She emphasized the name, then waited, staring at me as if I should intuit the importance of this information.

"I'm drawing a blank, Gram. Help me understand why I need to know this."

She let out a sigh. "The Carsons. Judge Carson. His son, Zachary, is married to—"

The light bulb came on. "Aha! Married to Charity Gordon! Charity Carson now. Doctor Charity Carson."

Gram grinned at me. "Bingo!"

"Okay, I get the connection to the Gordons, but why is this important?"

"Greta Bullfinch lived in. Full-time. She told her sister, who told her husband, who told Velma something."

"Gram, could you please just tell me what you heard?"

"Well," she said with great fanfare, "you won't believe it!"

"Arggh! Please! What won't I believe?"

She lowered her voice and leaned toward me. "The Carsons have a secret."

"What is it?"

"Well, I don't know that. Just that there is a secret of some kind."

"Big deal. Every family has secrets."

"This one is big. A real whopper, Velma said."

"Let me get this straight. Velma told you that her brother told her that his wife told him that her sister, the housekeeper, told her that the Carson family has a secret. But Greta, the housekeeper, didn't tell her sister, who didn't tell her husband, who didn't tell his sister Velma, who didn't tell you exactly what the secret is. Is that right?"

Gram nodded. "Exactly. Isn't that something?"

I smiled. "Yeah, Gram, that's something. But the something that it is, is nothing."

Gram frowned. "You need to investigate it. That's the point. It's a whatchamacallit—a lead!" She seemed so proud of herself that I couldn't burst her bubble.

"Okay, Gram. I'll dig around and see if I can find anything."

"You promise?"

I extended my little finger. "Pinky swear," I said.

She grabbed my pinky with hers and grinned so big, her little blue eyes practically disappeared behind her cheekbones.

I anticipated it being a huge waste of my time, digging into some secret mysterious something somewhere at some time. And it would probably turn out to be absolutely nothing.

CHAPTER NINETEEN

L ATER, I LAY IN the big soft pink bed in the Rose Room—so
called because of the pink-rosed wallpaper. Chloe was curled
next to me, asleep. The window AC unit blew cool relief in my
direction as I stared at the fake, Tiffany-style light fixture above
me, its colorful panels shining softly in the dim light of the
bedside lamp.

I thought about what Gram had told me about Greta
Bullfinch. I thought about the way we divide in this world—
the hill-dwellers and the flatlanders. Upper class. Working class.
The haves and the have-nots. Those who have real Tiffany and
those who have fakes.

We're not the Pemberleys, the Carsons, or the Kiplings.
Those families are the clean-ees.

Families like mine are the clean-ers. We don't *have* house-
keepers. We *are* housekeepers.

I'd had a conversation recently with a trash collector, who
told me I'd be amazed how much you can find out from people's

garbage. Maids, housekeepers, and gardeners would have similar knowledge. They'd know the secrets. Who drinks what, and how much. Who is cheating on whom. What's hidden in the closets, figuratively and literally. Who wears the real designer stuff, and who wears the knockoffs.

West Hill women are designer-dressed. I'm a knockoff kind of gal myself.

My older sister Stephanie, the fancy-schmancy investment adviser, drapes herself in designer duds. She's become a clean-ee.

She wasn't always, of course. She told me that she was at a lunch meeting at a hotel with her boss and the rest of the company early in her career. After the meal was done, she started to get up to help the wait staff clear the tables. An impulse arising from her roots among the cleaners of the world.

She said her boss grabbed her arm and pulled her back to sitting. "What are you doing?" he said. "Let these people do *their* job, and you do *yours!*"

She told me it was one of those "Huzzah!" moments in life when you realize you're no longer who you used to be.

I stroked Chloe's back. Had I had moments like that? I got my bachelor's degree, then worked as an administrative assistant at a local mental health clinic. Underachieving, my mother had said. "You deserve better," she'd told me often.

After my divorce, I'd worked for Trip—another administrative position—and heard again from my mother that I deserved better.

I thought that job might lead to a career for me—a career like Stephanie's maybe—but Trip's dad shut the operation down before anything could develop.

Now I was an office manager. Temporarily.

Chloe stood up and stretched, then looked into my eyes. "Chloe, when do I get my turn? When do I get to say, 'Huzzah! I've arrived!'"

She stretched forward and kicked up one back leg, then the other, before jumping off the bed and sauntering out into the hallway.

I turned off the bedside lamp and settled into the darkness. Maybe my "huzzah" would come with the email from the state saying I'd passed the investigator exam. Snarky snarked, *Pretty pathetic to need a piece of paper to tell you who you are.*

I thought of Maisie's death report—the finality of that paper. We start with our birth certificate, end with the death certificate. And in between, other "papers" testify to our existence. A high school diploma, maybe a college degree. Papers. Citizenship papers for some. Maybe a professional license. A certificate of achievement. So much time and energy spent working for and waiting for a piece of paper that will legitimize us, attest to the world that we know stuff.

To be able to wave it around and say, "I've arrived, and look! I have proof!"

Pathetic. Snarky had a point. I was waiting for the official word from the state to call myself an investigator. An *official* investigator. Until then, I was going to feel like an impostor.

Until then, my mother would probably keep telling me I deserve more, deserve better. Although, since she met Duncan, she'd been telling me far less often that I was underachieving. Now that she and Duncan were through, would her anxious attention shift back to me?

At least she seemed to approve of Nick Milcross as a potential boyfriend for me. I sank deeper into the soft bed, thinking about Nick, how nice it might be to dream about him.

But other thoughts intruded. If sister Stephanie still lived in Three Rivers, she'd simply *have* to live on the West Hill. That led to thoughts of the people on the Hill, to Maisie and her sister, and their mother, and the sad house they lived in.

The sadness that made her write, "It's all too much." Seeing that copy of the actual note attached to the police report, in a young girl's handwriting, made it all the more real.

I drifted off, wondering what she meant.

CHAPTER TWENTY

Thursday, June 27

JUST BEFORE TEN ON Thursday morning, I headed to the Gordons' house to pick up the yearbook before heading to the office.

If you've never been to Three Rivers, it's hard to imagine how opulent the West Hill is compared to the rest of the town. Driving up the wide, curving street, signs on either side let you know you are entering "West Hill Estates."

Vast, rolling, green lawns front the nice homes set well back from the road. Those nice homes give way to nicer homes, increasingly nicer the higher up you go. Tansy Pemberley's huge family home—a mansion, in my opinion—is at the top of the Hill. The house where Trip grew up is next door, separated from the Pemberleys by a few acres of lawn and a thick stand of tall pines. On the other side of the Pemberleys, the Carson family lives. More acreage and a long wall made of huge boulders divides them. Privacy for all.

I reached the Gordon house, about halfway up the Hill. *Crusty but not upper-crusty,* Snarky concluded. The two-story house had a wide porch, double garage, and a lawn full of dandelions. The paint on the window trim, on closer inspection, was peeling in spots. For Mrs. Gordon these days, breathing obviously took precedence over home maintenance.

I parked Cricket on the wide driveway and walked to the front door. Rang the bell. Nothing. Rang again. After several minutes, the door opened a crack. Mrs. Gordon recognized me and swung the door wider.

"Come in. Sorry I took so long. I was resting." She looked even paler than when I'd seen her on Tuesday. Her breathing was labored. "I have the yearbook for you." She led the way down a long hall to a den with a ton of bookshelves. A hospital bed stood in the middle of the room. The small table next to the bed held a lamp and a half-dozen prescription bottles.

She pointed to a cardboard box on a table in the corner of the room. "There's the yearbook and some other things of Maisie's that might be of help to you. You're welcome to take the box, but please bring it back."

I assured her I would.

She said, "You can see Maisie's room if you want. First door on the left, top of the stairs." She took a shuddering breath. "I'd show you, but—"

"That's all right. I really don't want to intrude." I didn't say what I meant, that it kind of creeped me out to think about visiting the bedroom of a dead girl.

"No intrusion. Maybe you can find something that will help." She sat on the edge of the hospital bed. "There is just one other thing."

"What's that, Mrs. Gordon?"

"Please find Maisie's birthstone necklace. I'd like to have it buried with me. I hope that doesn't sound too macabre."

"Not at all," I said. Who was I to judge a dying mother? This was her grieving heart's cry to have a final connection with her daughter. "I'll try my best to find it."

She sighed and slumped back against the pillows. "When you're done upstairs, please show yourself out? I'm exhausted. Going to your office sapped me, I'm afraid." She shot me a last plaintive look. "Find out what really happened to my daughter? Please?"

Anxious Me cautioned, *Don't make promises you can't keep.*

Kinder, Gentler Me whispered, *Tell the poor woman what she needs to hear.*

I chose the middle ground. "I'll do my best."

With a whispered, "Thank you," she closed her eyes.

I took the box and headed up the stairs to Maisie's bedroom. My footsteps echoed on the wooden staircase. I set the box of Maisie's things on the floor outside her bedroom door. I took a deep breath, opened the door, and stepped inside.

There are no ghosts, I know, but there's something. Something that makes us feel connected to someone somewhere else. Sometimes, you enter a space and have that feeling that you're not alone.

Maisie was everywhere in that room. Posters on the wall of the two boy bands popular in those days—Wammer Jammer and Bad Boyz—screamed fifteen-year-old girl. I was sure she'd chosen the pink-and-white gingham bedspread and the matching curtains.

I pictured Maisie sitting on the little stool with the ruffle in front of the vanity with the large mirror. I imagined her hand holding the lipstick and writing the letter B, then drawing the heart around it. There it was, just as Mrs. Gordon had described.

The room was dust-free. Mrs. Gordon was probably still cleaning it, despite her failing health.

I walked to the small white desk with two drawers in the corner of the room. A ceramic cup in the shape of a cat held pencils and pens. I pictured Maisie sitting in the little white chair, doing her homework, writing in her journal, singing along with the boys in the band.

I opened one drawer. I flipped through the homework papers—all A's and B's. Good student. Smart girl.

In the second drawer, under more homework papers, I found a half-dozen letters with a ribbon tied around them. They were addressed to Maisie in a woman's hand, with a return address in The City.

I scanned the first letter. News of the day—comments about the weather and gardening. Questions for Maisie about school and family events. The letter was signed: "Love, Grandma."

The rest of the letters were much the same. I retied the ribbon and set them back in the drawer.

Maisie had a maternal grandfather in The City, the man who had hired Sheena. Was this "grandma" his wife? Maybe Maisie had written to her grandmother, maybe told her things she didn't tell her mother. Maybe Grandma could offer me some insight into Maisie's state of mind before she died.

I opened the door of the closet. Empty. I paused, imagining having to clear out Gram's closet one day or my mother having to clear mine. Such a personal thing going through someone else's clothing. Someone you loved. How difficult for a parent.

I stepped away from the closet. The floor creaked underfoot. I pulled back the edge of the pink area rug and felt around the edges of the hardwood planks, hoping for a secret compartment. Perhaps Maisie hid a secret diary there, a diary that would explain why she killed herself.

No such luck. No loose planks. No secrets.

I lifted the twin bed mattress and ran my hand over the box spring on all the edges of the bed. Nothing hidden there either.

I crossed to the one window in the room and looked out over the backyard. A roof under the window extended out over what I assumed was a back porch. Was Maisie the kind of teenager who would sneak out at night? Perhaps to meet a mystery someone with the initial B?

I stood contemplating that possibility when someone behind me cleared their throat. I turned. The woman, about my height and build, had hard lines around her mouth and streaks of gray in her dark hair.

"My mother told me you were up here." She came across the room.

I offered my hand. "You must be Charity. I'm Mackenzie Prentice." We shook, her grip cool, firm, and confident.

She waved a hand around the room. "Sad, isn't it? My mother let me take the clothes, but she wouldn't let me change anything else in here. She comes up here every day. Well, she did that until recently. She's not well, you know?"

I nodded understanding.

"After Maisie died, she'd come up here and just sit. Day after day. Just sitting, staring into space. Major depression for a long time. She got a little better, but now, with the cancer, she's worse than ever. Doesn't go outside. You've seen the lawn. What a mess. Can't imagine what the neighbors are thinking. So embarrassing."

I said nothing, but I imagined that the neighbors might be compassionate toward a widow who'd lost her husband, then her daughter, and was now dying of cancer.

I watched as Charity crossed the room to the desk. She took a pink pen with a fuzzy pink pompom attached to the eraser end from the ceramic cup. "Maisie loved stuff like this. Loved pink." Her fingers played through the pompom. She smiled. "I can still see her at this desk, writing in her diary."

"There were some letters in the drawer there. From your grandmother in The City to Maisie. Is that your mother's mother?"

She wrinkled her nose. "Yes. Our other grandparents—on our dad's side—died when we were little. Maisie and Grandma Margaret were very close. They wrote letters back and forth. It was so sad when Grandma passed. That was the year before Maisie died. She loved Maisie." Her voice got soft. "Everybody loved Maisie."

Charity returned the pen to the cup and walked back to the window. She crossed her arms and stared outside. "Maisie was always writing. Should have grown up to be a novelist."

"She liked to read romances too? I noticed some in the box your mother gave me. And some spiral notebooks."

"Probably notes for romance novels. She had a vivid imagination."

I pointed at the vanity mirror. "What about that heart on the mirror? You have any idea who B is?"

"Nope. She never talked to me about it." She pointed to the backyard. "Just look at that mess out there. I've tried to help my mother keep things up. Paid for gardeners. Hired a housekeeper for her. She fired them all, said it was all a waste of money." Charity sighed. "I begged her to sell the house and start over in a new place. She wouldn't hear of it. My husband, Zach, and I offered to have her live with us, but she wouldn't even consider it. She stays in this house, as if she's expecting Maisie or my dad to walk back in someday. It's pathetic, really."

"Grief can be very difficult," I said. "Some people just give up."

Charity snorted. "This is beyond grieving. This is psycho."

I frowned. That seemed a bit harsh.

She said quickly, "That's not an official diagnosis. It's just crazy that she's locked herself away like this. I love her and want her to be happy. Really, I do."

"I'm sure you do. People handle grief in their own way," I said and shifted gears. "By the way, do you have any idea what happened to your sister's birthstone necklace?"

Charity tossed her head. "Oh. My. God. Did she ask you to find it?"

"She did, yes."

She scowled. "Why in the hell is she so obsessed with that stupid necklace? She had me looking for it forever after Maisie died. I can't tell you how many times she asked me to go up to that stupid cliff and look again." She paused, then ranted on. "Did she tell you why she wants it?"

Before I could answer, Charity said, voice rising, "She wants to be buried with it! My God! She just won't let it go!"

I kept my voice calm. "I can understand her wanting that last connection with your sister."

She shot me a look. "Oh, trust me, they were connected. *Way* connected. Whatever Maisie wanted, she got. My mother spoiled her rotten. And made me take care of her, always watching out for her precious little darling—" She stopped and took a breath. "I mean, don't get me wrong. I loved my little sister, and I certainly didn't want her to die. It was just that—" She looked out the window.

I waited, then prompted, "Just that . . . ?"

Calm now, her voice quiet, she said, "Just that my mother favored Maisie. That's all. Preferred her. She never said it out loud, but you know. You just know."

I remembered what Mrs. Gordon had said about their father being disappointed that Maisie was a second daughter. Maybe the mother tried to make up for that, and Charity felt that as favoritism. Who knows?

I thought about my relationship with my four siblings. We had our squabbles, as all children do. Our mother, single and working full-time, didn't have the time or energy to play favorites. She jokes that she ignored us all equally, and that's why we turned out okay. We all get along fine now as adults.

I felt a pang of sympathy for Charity Gordon. "I'm sorry. That must have been hard for you."

Charity looked at me and shrugged. "Ancient history. Did you find what you were looking for? If so, I'll walk you out."

Since I didn't know what I was looking for, I couldn't say whether I'd found it or not. I went into the hall and picked up the box of Maisie's things. Charity closed the bedroom door, and we walked downstairs together.

She headed toward the den. "I'm going to check on my mom. Good luck," she said with a little wave.

"Thanks," I said. The front door latched loudly as I closed it behind me.

CHAPTER TWENTY-ONE

I WAS EAGER TO GET on with my investigation. I texted Chief Bronson from the car, asking for help in finding Officer Burling, listed as the primary on Maisie's death investigation report.

Five minutes later, the chief called me with the address. "Just talked to him. He'll be expecting you."

Officer Harlan Burling buzzed me into the two-story brick apartment building on the south side of town. The hallway held decades of cooking smells.

He stood in the open doorway of apartment 205.

"Officer Burling, I presume." I shook hands with the heavy-set man. Five ten, maybe two-fifty. His short-sleeved, Hawaiian-print shirt stretched over his substantial belly, buttons gaping above his navel. Bald. Long scar under his left eye. Barefoot. Hairy toes.

Good job noticing the details, Rational congratulated me.

Especially the hairy toes. Very important. Snarky can be *so* sarcastic.

"Call me Harlan, please. Chief said you'd be coming by. Come in."

I walked into the stuffy apartment. A threadbare recliner in brown and orange plaid pointed toward a gigantic TV screen. The small table beside the recliner held an ashtray full of cigarette butts and two empty beer cans. Several water rings marked the tabletop. The ancient-looking window air conditioner did little to cool the room or dissipate the smell of stale smoke and old beer.

He pointed to the worn couch. "Have a seat. Can I get you a beer? Or a soda?"

"Just water?"

He went to the kitchen, giving me time to look around. Two plaques on the wall recognized him for his service on the police department. A collage frame held family photos—his children and, I assumed, grandchildren.

He came back, handed me the glass of water, then sat in the recliner. He flicked a Zippo lighter and lit a Marlboro. Inhaled, exhaled.

I sat, set the glass on the coffee table, and pointed at the collage. "Nice family," I said.

He told me about his three children and his five grandchildren. Told me how his wife of forty years had died two years before from pancreatic cancer. How his son in Arizona was trying to get him to move there. How he was considering the idea. "Nothing much to do here anymore but watch sports and cry in your beer, ya know?"

"I'm sorry for your loss," I said. "Arizona is nice." *Make small talk, establish rapport, put the subject at ease.* Just the way the chief taught me.

"Too hot for my taste. I mean, Jesus, this place gets hot, too, but it doesn't go all year. I'm not sure I'm cut out to be a desert rat."

I sipped the tepid water, then said, "So I'm working with the chief on an old case."

"I figured you weren't here to talk about the weather. It's the Gordon case, right? After the chief called, I dug out my old scrapbook." He gestured to a book on the coffee table, reached forward, and opened it. "I kept the news stories and other stuff from my cases over the years. Every once in a while, I look at it all, for old times' sake. Used to drive my wife crazy."

He gave a sad smile, then turned the book so I could see the front-page article from the local newspaper, *The Daily Bulletin*, known affectionately as *The Bull*.

He leaned back in the recliner as I read the headline aloud. "'Local teen falls from cliff.'" I scanned the article. "Just says she fell. What do you think?"

"Everybody assumed it was suicide."

"But you were on the case. I want to know what *you* think."

"Could have been." He paused. "Or it could have been something else. Hard to say. And impossible to say after all these years."

"You have doubts?"

He heaved a sigh and looked out the window. He took a drag off the cigarette and then met my eyes. "Yeah. Just the way it was shoved aside. My supervisor at the time—Sergeant Archer—told me after a couple of days to sign off and move on."

He took another drag and exhaled. "Archer's gone now. Heart attack." He shook his head. "He was a good guy. Anyway, I wasn't anywhere near ready to close the case, but he ordered me to do it."

"Any theories on that? Why he was in such a hurry?"

"Well, I guess because she left that note."

"Cryptic, wasn't it? 'It's all too much' could mean a lot of things."

He nodded. "True, but Archer said we didn't have the manpower. He needed us all freed up because we had a crime wave going on right then. A lot of drug traffic coming through town, between Chicago and The City, and a couple other high-profile cases affecting some of the rich folks in town. Maybe Sarge was taking heat from higher up—his boss, or maybe the mayor taking heat from his cronies. Who knows? I was just a lowly officer trying to do my job. I gave in."

"Maisie's mother is dying. Cancer. She came to me because she doesn't believe her daughter died by suicide. You were there. Do you have anything you can give me that might help this poor woman get the answers she needs?"

He leaned back, drew in the last of the cigarette, and closed his eyes. When he opened them, he exhaled and squashed the butt into the ashtray. He leaned toward me. "There was something about a necklace. A cross or something. The mother was frantic. I figured it was the grief."

"Yes, a cross with a ruby in the center. The girl's birthstone. Maisie's mother is hoping I can find it now. It wasn't on her when her body was found, right?" I remembered the photos of the scene.

"That's right. We went back and searched the scene but didn't find it. Frankly, it didn't seem important. The dead—uh, the girl could have lost it anywhere. And, like I said, I had orders to close the file. End of story."

We chatted for another half an hour about other cases as Harlan showed me his scrapbook. Then I thanked him and left my card with the usual "just in case you remember anything else" spiel.

"End of story," he'd said.

Maybe it was. Maybe not.

I stepped out into the heat. I checked the weather app on my phone. The air temperature was ninety-three. "Hotter than a pistol," Gram would say. I hoped she and Nathan were staying cool.

I wiped the sweat off my forehead as I walked around the corner to where I'd parked Cricket.

Sheena was leaning against my car, smoking. She saw me and ground the cigarette under her heel. "So, Miss Office Manager, what did Officer Burling have to say?"

Just slap her. I ignored Snarky. Too hot for a street fight. "How did you—"

She held up her hand. "Cut the crap. He was on the case. I saw the file. Now, are you going to tell me what he had to say, or am I going to have to tattle on you? Tell Trip you're not cooperating?"

Badass: *Don't tell the witch anything!*

Snarky: *Just slap her. You know you want to. Go ahead!*

Anxious: *But she'll tell Trip we've been withholding, and he'll get mad.* Anxious still feels like she felt in elementary school—always scared of getting in trouble.

Rational: *Maisie's mother is running out of time. Sheena has experience. Cooperate with her. Get this thing figured out, for Mrs. Gordon's sake.*

I sighed and surrendered to my own wisdom. "He said he was ordered to close the case early. Other pressing priorities for the department at the time."

She gave a knowing nod. "Yeah, that happens. So frustrating when you can't take the time to really investigate. There's always more for cops to do." She looked around and wrinkled her nose. "Even in a place like this."

The snot. I mimicked her tone. "A place like this? We might not be the big city, but, yeah, even here. People do bad things. Imagine that."

"You know what I mean," Sheena said. "You gonna tell me what he said or not?"

I exhaled, let it go. "Burling said there was some big deal at the time—drugs or a scandal of some sort. He wasn't specific. But it was enough that Maisie's death got ignored. Official cause of death was suicide. End of story."

"You should have invited me to come along. I could have gotten more out of him. You know? Cop to cop?"

"I'm sure you would have done things *so* much better, Sheena. I'm sure you would have gotten information that nobody but God knows! I'm sure you could have just worked your little magic spell all over the guy, just like you've done with Trip. I'm sure—" I stopped.

She was smiling. "You really don't like me, do you, Prentice? I'm just a giant pain in your ass. A thorn in your side, right? Right?" She leaned toward me. I'd seen that look of challenge before.

We stared at each other for a couple of beats.

Rational Me said, *Drop the rope.* Gram's advice when you find yourself in a verbal tug-of-war with someone. *Drop the rope.*

I made a fist and extended it toward her chest.

She flinched and took a half-step back. "What are you doing?"

I smiled, then opened my hand. "Dropping the rope." I gave a little wave. "See ya!" I walked around my car and got behind the wheel.

Sheena yelled, "Whatever!" as I drove away.

CHAPTER TWENTY-TWO

NOBODY WAS IN THE office when I got back to TriMak. I assumed Trip was attending the Thursday noon meeting of the Lions Club. The chief was who-knows-where. I peeked into the middle office. Evidence of Sheena's occupation of the space —*my* space—was everywhere. *Ugh*. No sign of her or Germany.

I made a coffee and sat at my desk. I opened Charity Gordon's senior yearbook. Nostalgic. There was Miss Madigan, the math teacher I'd had for tenth-grade algebra. Ancient, prim, hair in a bun, sturdy shoes. Her rules. Sit up straight. Raise your hand. And absolutely, positively, no gum.

I heard her voice. "Somebody is chewing gum. I can smell it!" The room would get very quiet. Miss Madigan ordered the offender, "Take your gum out into the hall at once and dispose of it! I do not want it smelling up my classroom!"

Miss Madigan was the embodiment of every strict teacher, every old-school disciplinarian. I googled her, found her obituary. Long live Miss Madigan.

I continued examining the pictures. Mr. Simonson, the economics teacher, taught us the right way to buy a car: "Never buy brand-new," still rings in my head. Heaven forbid I should ever lose a gazillion dollars in depreciation just driving a brand-new car off the showroom floor.

Miss Peters, the girls' gym teacher. She didn't like me much. I never could climb the stupid rope. I stunk at volleyball. Not my thing. I faked my mother's signature on notes to get excused from gym class a lot. Miss Peters never seemed to notice that I "had cramps" every week and a half.

Miss Harada was great for English. I looked at Mrs. Boswick's picture, standing in her biology classroom. I smelled formaldehyde, remembered the frog corpses splayed out on the table. *Dead stuff. Ugh.*

So many memories. I needed to focus on Maisie. Maybe her teachers would remember something that would help my investigation. I looked through the box Mrs. Gordon had given me and found Maisie's report cards with her teachers listed. Mr. Market had died ten years ago, but the others were, according to my online sources, still living. Most had local addresses.

I thought about seeing my old teachers. Part of me hoped to hear, "I'm proud of you, Mackenzie." Can we ever get too much of that? My older brother Greg and sister Stephanie had heard plenty of praise in school. Younger brother Robbie was funny and popular, and baby sister Deanne was in all the right activities. Praise, praise, praise.

Me? Not so much. I'd floated through school, average student, average everything.

I continued to page through the yearbook. The popular cheerleaders and jocks. The musical band geeks. The brainiacs in the science club, language clubs, National Honor Society, forensics, and on the school paper. And the performers in the school play, dance line, and show choir.

Is every high school the same? There are those successful, involved go-getters, and then there are the rest of us. Bumbling along, behaving ourselves, for the most part, just making it through.

I scanned the names under each group picture. I found Maisie Gordon sitting in the first row of the band. Nothing stood out. Ordinary girl in a white blouse and black skirt. Clarinet across her lap. I added three band boys with B names to my list.

I paged past a section of group shots, homerooms pictured together under the caption "Next Year's Grads." The juniors.

The sophomore homerooms were grouped under "Future Upperclassmen." How recently—just twenty years ago—we defaulted to the masculine, as in police*men*, fire*men*, post*men*. Now, thanks to demands for more gender equality, we have police *officers*, fire*fighters*, and postal *workers*.

I found Maisie Gordon in Miss Harada's sophomore homeroom 310. Seated third from the right, in the front row of the color picture, M. Gordon wore a white blouse with a brown-and-yellow plaid, V-neck sweater over it. Her brownish hair hung straight and nondescript. No braids, no clips, no fancy anything. Plain.

She posed awkwardly, one shoulder hunched, unsmiling. A teenaged girl, self-conscious. That teenaged angsty feeling. *Don't look at me. Don't judge me, please.*

She looked away from the camera, down to her right. What was she thinking about? An upcoming history test? The boy she called "B," whoever he was?

What happened to you, Maisie Gordon? You never got your senior pictures taken. Never went to prom. Never wore a cap and gown. Never...

Stop! Rational Me knew I was heading down a long, sad path. *You're gonna cry all over the yearbook. Pull it together!*

I needed to focus on figuring out what really happened and not waste time on what could have been.

I got myself another cup of coffee, then sat back in my chair. I unwrapped an Almond Joy from the stash in my desk drawer. Caffeine. Sugar. Great combination.

As I sipped and chewed, I found Jemma Dalworthy in her homeroom picture. In the back row, tall, pretty, with long dark hair, well-dressed, smiling confidently. She appeared again in the volleyball team photo above the caption "District Champs!"

Onyx Lyden was in the same homeroom as Jemma and also in the choir. Onyx, in the middle row, had curly red hair, freckles, and glasses.

I flipped toward the end of the book to the senior pictures. There was Charity Gordon, shoulder-length dark hair in the smooth style so popular in the day, an expensive-looking white knit top, and a pendant at her neck. A cross with a tiny golden stone. Her birthstone necklace.

I flipped back to Maisie's homeroom picture. It was hard to see the details, so I took a photo with my phone, then zoomed in. Maisie's matching cross, with the red stone, was around her neck.

I flipped to the sports team pictures in the yearbook. Could Maisie's mysterious someone be one of the jocks? I made a list in my computer of the boys with B names. Brent, Brad, Brady. And there were a couple of Roberts—maybe Bobs—as well.

I scanned the football teams. Each senior player had an individual picture, like the kind they could imagine having on a trading card when they'd be playing pro ball in the future. I scanned the junior varsity squad and the basketball team. I added a Brett and a Bernardo to the list and others from the hockey, track, and baseball teams. Ben, Blake, Bart, and Boone.

The list of B boys was long. This was going to take forever.

Must be a way to narrow this down, Rational Me suggested. I dug through the rest of the box Mrs. Gordon had given me. Flipped the pages of the several paperback romance novels. Nothing flew out. Paged through Maisie's homework assignments. No notes, no doodling. Just homework.

I scanned the pages of the notebooks. A lot of "once upon a time" stuff, stories, dreams, and fantasies. Some of it might be about her mystery boy, but there was nothing like, "B and I kissed in the stairwell at school today." Nothing so obvious.

No pages pouring out her teenaged problems. No sign that this young girl was depressed. But no sign that she wasn't either.

I was getting nowhere fast. And I was sick of sitting at my desk.

It was time to talk with Maisie's friends.

CHAPTER TWENTY-THREE

M Y ONLINE SEARCH SHOWED no Jemma Dalworthy in Three Rivers. A couple Jemma Dalworthys lived in other parts of the country. Did I want to see addresses and phone numbers? Criminal records?

We have no real privacy anymore.

After a few minutes, I knew Jemma Dalworthy of Three Rivers had married Steven Provost fifteen years ago. No criminal records for either.

His name seemed familiar. I checked the yearbook. He was in Charity Gordon's senior class and was on the football team.

I'd learned that Jemma and Steven had four children, the youngest's birth record dated just four months prior.

The Provosts lived in Campbell, a tiny town a half hour south of Three Rivers. Their address started with a letter and then numbers—a "fire number" address common in rural areas.

I popped the address into my phone's GPS. The air felt

heavy as I stepped outside. As predicted, the humidity was high and the temperature over ninety degrees.

Thirty-five minutes later, with Cricket blasting cool air all the way, I rolled past the mailbox with PROVOST and the correct fire number, up the long driveway toward an old double-wide mobile home.

Black-eyed Susans filled a flower bed along the front of the house. Gram has them in the garden at the Victorian. Sturdy little perennial daisies. Yellow faces. Black hearts.

I knocked. A tall boy about twelve opened the door. He was barefoot, wearing shorts and a tee shirt with the solar system printed on it.

"Is your mom home?"

He turned and yelled, "Mom! Someone's here!" He sat on the couch and resumed a video game he'd been playing on the flat-screen TV in the corner. I waited in the doorway, listening to the window air conditioner working hard to cool the place. The unit made a pinging noise every few seconds.

A minute later, Jemma Dalworthy Provost came from the back of the house, carrying an infant in her arms. The baby wore only a diaper.

Jemma was a few inches taller than my five-foot-six, slim, with dark hair pulled into a bun. She wore cut-off jean shorts and a black tank top with a picture of a gone-to-seed dandelion on it and the words GO WITH THE FLOW. From what I could see, Jemma was in great shape, especially since she'd just had a baby.

A boy, maybe two-ish, with long blond curls, clung to her bare leg and gave me a wary look. Jemma directed the older boy, "Bubba, turn that game off and take your brother. You and Cole go play in the back with Georgie."

The older boy pried the toddler off her leg and disappeared into the back of the trailer.

"You're Jemma Dalworthy?"

"Provost now," she said. She smiled, revealing incredibly white teeth. The house might be run-down, but her teeth were going to be well-maintained.

I introduced myself and handed her my card. "I'm investigating Maisie Gordon's death."

"Come on in." She gestured to the sagging couch. "Have a seat."

I sat and looked around at the wood-paneled walls. A table with a dozen sad-looking plants sat in front of the window. On the far wall, a crucifix.

Jemma spread a blanket on the worn carpet and laid the baby on it, set a couple of plastic toys in front of her. "Tummy time for Annie," Jemma said.

"Three boys and a girl? You have your hands full," I said.

"More than full," she said with a weary smile. She offered me a Diet Coke. I declined. She sat in a recliner across the room. "What's to investigate? Maisie killed herself. End of story."

I explained that her family wanted to be sure. "I know it was a long time ago. What do you remember?"

Jemma screwed up her face. "It's been a long time, yes. We were best friends, Maisie, Onyx, and I."

"Onyx Lyden?"

Jemma nodded.

"I'll want to talk to her as well. Do you have a number for her?"

"I don't, but she's still a nurse at the hospital, as far as I know. Haven't been in touch for years now." She gestured with her head toward the back room. "Having them ties you down, you know?"

I didn't know, but I nodded anyway. "Jemma, did Maisie seem depressed to you? Did she ever talk about harming herself?"

Jemma looked up at the ceiling, frowned, then met my eyes. "We all had the usual teenager stuff, I suppose. The self-harming, you know. Cutting a little, burning a little. Starving ourselves to be skinnier. That was the big thing back then. That and trying alcohol and pills."

I thought about these girls living in the opulence of the West Hill, having all the amenities of life, the pools, the cars, the clothes. And still self-harming. Why did they need to do that? Was life so awful?

Jemma continued as if she read my mind. "I look back and wonder why we thought life was so miserable. We had it great back then." She looked around the living room of the mobile home. "It's a long fall from the top of the Hill to this."

I waited.

She shook her head. "This is what I get for marrying for love instead of money." Her brows went up. "Don't get me wrong. Steve's a great guy, and I wouldn't trade for anything. But I think about what I gave up to marry him." Her voice took on a bitter undertone. "My family cut me off without a dime. My parents have never once come here. They don't care about me or my family. What kind of grandparents don't care about their grandchildren?"

"Sorry. I can't imagine how much that must hurt."

She gave a dismissive wave. "Whatever. I'm over it now. But I feel bad for my kids."

"They seem like nice kids." I told her about my nephews, Joey and Charlie. "Joey is twelve. About the age of your oldest?"

"Yes, Bryce is twelve. He's usually out with his dad, working in the summer. But I needed him home today."

"What does your husband do?"

"Steve is a carpenter, and Bryce loves to help him. I don't know how much help the boy can be, but it's a father-son thing." She smiled.

"That's sweet," I said. "Back to Maisie, what do you remember? Anything at all. Some insignificant detail might matter. You never know."

Jemma described the fun the girls had together growing up on the Hill. Pool parties and sleepovers at her house, giggling about boys.

I said, "She might have had a crush on somebody with the initial B. Any idea who it was?"

"Oh yeah, she had a huge crush, but she wouldn't tell me or Onyx who it was. We named every boy in class whose name started with a B. She just kept saying, 'Nope. Not him.' We even tried to tickle-torture her, but she wouldn't tell." Jemma smiled at the memory, then turned solemn. "That was a week before she died."

I was just about to ask her about being the last person to see Maisie alive when the baby started crying.

"Duty calls," Jemma said, then sighed. "Or, in this case, duty cries." She picked the baby up just as we heard a crash from the back of the trailer. "Oh Lord! Now what?" She hurried toward the back room as she called over her shoulder. "See yourself out, okay?"

She disappeared before I could thank her and ask her to call or text if she thought of anything else. I picked up my card from where she'd dropped it on the baby's blanket and left it on the end of the cluttered kitchen counter.

I drove away from the house thinking about Jemma "falling from the hill." And parents who could reject a child like that. My grandmother would never ignore her grandchildren. And my mother was a doting grandmother to all my siblings' children.

If money could create a divide like that in a family, I was glad I grew up poor.

CHAPTER TWENTY-FOUR

B ACK AT THE OFFICE, I waved hello to the chief, who was at
his desk, tying more flies. Up front, Germany was sitting at
my desk. "Hey, Germ. What's up? Where's your boss?"

"She and Trip left. Something about showing her something at his house."

I'll bet, Snarky whispered. "And you're at *my* desk. Why?"

"I just thought I'd sit here in case anyone came in."

"Did anyone come in?"

Germany nodded. "A little girl. She asked if"—he air quoted—"the 'detective lady' found her banjo yet."

Geez. Louisa. I'd forgotten about her. "I'm hoping she'll forget about the bird."

Germany said, "Fat chance. She'll be one of those who asks
you every day for a status update. Some clients are like that,
aren't they? Sheena's had a few who got super annoying."

I told Germany about a previous worried mother who'd
harassed me mercilessly until I found her son. My turn to air
quote. "Her 'missing boy' was a man, in his thirties, living with

his girlfriend." I shifted gears. "I need to do a search. Mind if I use my computer?"

His cheeks pinked. "Sorry." He shifted to the chair next to my desk.

I opened the software and turned the laptop toward him. "Look familiar?"

He looked at the screen. "Nope. Sheena doesn't let me do this kind of thing."

"Let me show you how it's done."

He grinned, scooted his chair next to mine, and leaned in.

In half a second, we knew a lot about Onyx Lyden. No recent photos, just a copy of her senior class picture.

"Whoa! How'd you do all that so fast?"

"Magic. Push a button and voilà!" I said, to cover the fact that I had no idea how the software really worked, just that it did.

I'd hoped for even more information, but Onyx Lyden was evidently the one person in the world not on Facebook or any other social media.

"We've got her address, and she drives a Mercedes," I said and sent the screenshot to the printer behind my desk.

Germany asked, "How does she afford that car? How much do nurses make?"

"A lot, depending on the job. Or maybe she saved up for it, or maybe it was a gift. Or maybe she just got a really good deal." I shut down my laptop. "Want to see if we can track this nurse down?"

Germany jumped up. "Heck, yeah!"

A very enthusiastic sidekick, indeed.

We drove to the hospital parking lot and cruised the aisles, looking for a Mercedes with the license plate our search had given us.

"There!" Germany pointed to a red car parked at the far end of the lot. "License plate says 86NURS."

I snapped a photo of the car with my phone. "So, Onyx Lyden must be inside working."

"How about leaving a note?"

"Good idea, Germ." I took out a card and wrote my personal cell number on the back with a note asking Onyx to call me about Maisie Gordon. Germany stuck the card under the driver's side windshield wiper of the Mercedes, then got back into Cricket.

He said, "Should we go inside and try to find her?"

"Another good idea, Germany. You're great at this stuff."

"Thanks," he said, blushing a little.

Our Lady of Mercy, a sprawling complex of buildings on the Wolf River, is the main hospital in this area of our state. Patients can have a lovely view of trees and water if they happen to luck out. The unlucky get the rooms with views of brick walls or the parking structure. I assume it's the luck of the draw and not based on wealth or the kind of insurance a patient has. I would hope the people who live "on the Hill" don't get preferential treatment. But given how life works, I'm probably being naive.

I walked to the lobby information desk. The woman at the desk had a nametag with GENEVIEVE VOLUNTEER on it.

"Is Volunteer your last name?"

She gave a half-smile. "Everyone asks me that."

My cheeks got hot. Snarky hissed, *You're hilarious. Not.* I said, "Sorry. I'm looking to speak to an employee. A nurse. Onyx Lyden. I know she's working. Can you just tell me where I can find her? I really need to talk with her."

"I'm sorry. Your best bet is to call the main hospital number. They can connect you if she's available."

I got serious. "It's very important that I speak with her." I stopped short of lying that it was an emergency, then gave her my most innocent smile. "I don't suppose you could give me her phone number?"

"You suppose correctly. I can't release any personal information."

Usually, people tell me all kinds of things. Not Ms. Volunteer at Our Lady of Mercy.

We turned away from the information desk, and Germany said, "Why don't we just look around the hospital? Maybe we can find her."

In high school, Onyx wore glasses and had a red mop of thick, curly hair. She was shorter than most of the girls around her in the choir picture, but I had no idea what Onyx Lyden looked like these days. "She's twenty years older now. Could be fatter or thinner. Could have had a growth spurt after tenth grade. Could have colored her hair. Gotten contacts," I said.

"Or become a man," Germany said.

Anything was possible.

CHAPTER TWENTY-FIVE

N OTHING MORE TO DO here," I said as we got back into
Cricket. "Do you want to have dinner at my grandmother's house tonight?" Gram has an open-door policy at
dinnertime. Always plenty of food. Anyone welcome anytime.
Just set another place.

Plus, I figured the boy could use a home-cooked meal. I
didn't see Sheena as the domestic goddess type, going all gour-
met in Trip's kitchen.

Germany didn't hesitate. "That would be great."

"We have one more stop to make."

I had asked Gram to ask Velma to ask her brother for Greta
Bullfinch's contact information. Gram had written Greta's
southside address and landline phone number on the back of
an old envelope.

Greta Bullfinch picked up on the second ring. I explained
who I was, and she said she'd be happy to meet with me. "I just
got home from my step aerobics class at the Y. I'll be outside in
the back garden."

Greta Bullfinch was active. I'd heard she was in her nineties. Step aerobics was impressive.

I parked Cricket on the street in front of the small ranch house on the south side of Three Rivers, on Maple Street, not far from Holy Assumption Catholic Church.

Along the block, ranch homes are interspersed with story-and-a-half Cape Cods, a typical mix of styles from the late 1940s to the 1970s. People in this pleasant neighborhood keep the grass cut and the litter picked up. They decorate for Halloween, put Christmas lights on their eaves in winter, and host summer barbecues with the neighbors on their backyard patios.

Greta Bullfinch's yard was tidy, just what you'd expect from a housekeeper. Trim bushes along the front foundation were interspersed with flower beds. I'm not much of a gardener, but I learned a lot as a child, helping Gram in her garden.

Roses climbed a trellis against the house. Bees visiting the echinacea ignored us as we headed down the sidewalk around the right side of the house to the backyard.

I called, "Miss Bullfinch?"

"Over here!" She waved a hand. She was kneeling on a foam rubber pad, pulling weeds. I hurried toward her to help her up. She stood quickly, refusing my offered hand. "No need, dear. I'm not one of those feeble old ladies," she said with a chuckle.

You know how a name conjures up an image? Greta Bull-finch. I expected her to be a large woman, formidable. A matron in a women's prison, maybe.

The opposite of that image stood before me. Greta Bull-finch was short—no more than five-foot-two, and looked to be, as Gram might say, "a hundred pounds, soaking wet." A green tee shirt over her denim shorts read, "I'm closer to God in my garden than anywhere else on earth."

She took off her gardening gloves and shook our hands. "Lovely to meet you both," she said. A straw sun hat with flowered fabric on the underside of the brim shaded her thin face.

"I like your hat," I said.

"It saves me from getting more wrinkles than I already have." Her laugh was lilting, pleasant.

"I know what you mean," I said.

She squinted at me. "Oh heavens! You're young, dear. You've got years before you need to worry about wrinkles. Now, let's get out of this heat," she said. She led us to the patio table on her back deck. An orange-and-white striped umbrella shaded the four chairs.

"Have a seat. I'll get us something cold to drink." She disappeared through the sliding glass door at the back of the house.

Germany and I sat on the orange-and-white striped cushions on her patio chairs, feeling a tad cooler under the umbrella.

I looked out at the neat yard. Tall hydrangea bushes stood along the back fence, their massive puffballs just starting to bloom. I recognized Joe Pye weed in a back corner. Like Gram's, this would yield massive lavender flower heads later in the summer.

The echinacea plants, with petals like ballet tutus surrounding brown pincushion centers, are also one of Gram's favorites.

Germany pointed. "What are those? They look like little goose heads."

"That's white loosestrife," I said. "My grandmother has some of that. Very invasive." I imitated Gram. "Watch out! They'll take over everything!"

Hollyhocks stood against the wooden fence to my right. A grapevine traversed the fence on the left. Posts held bird feeders of various sizes throughout the garden. Chickadees and nut-hatches flitted back and forth. A long, multi-perched feeder had attracted a whole crew of goldfinches.

"Dang. That's a lot of birds," Germany said.

I murmured agreement, watching several monarch butter-flies making their way among the butterfly weed and coreopsis.

Birds. Bees. Butterflies. Idyllic. Peaceful. *If I ever retire, I want to live like this,* Rational Me thought.

Snarky argued, *You'd be bored out of your skull in a week.* I told them both to be quiet.

Our hostess returned with a large tray holding three glasses of lemonade and a plate of yellow cookies with white frosting.

We sipped lemonade as Greta Bullfinch talked about her gardens and her lifelong love of growing things. "That's why I loved teaching in the elementary grades in The City. Help-ing children grow into the best people they can be. It's like gardening."

I bit into a cookie. "Mmm, these just melt in your mouth," I said.

Germany reached for a second one.

She smiled. "Yes. These are my lemon melt-aways. The Car-son boys loved them. They were Buddy's favorites." She paused, looked out at the garden.

Here was my opening. "Miss Bullfinch—"

She smiled and held up a hand. "Call me Greta, please. My sister told me what Velma told her about you. You're smart. And an investigator. My, oh my. Isn't that something? I don't think I've ever met one before."

I didn't want to tell her I wasn't official yet. Let her be impressed.

She continued. "I know you didn't come here to talk about cookies and gardening."

"That's true, Miss, uh, Greta. I wanted to ask you about your time working for the Carsons."

She smiled and relaxed back into her chair. "Such a lovely family. So many fond memories. I was there almost twenty years, you know."

She'd retired from teaching at fifty-two and moved to Three Rivers to help her sister take care of their aging mother. "I was sixty when our mother passed. I was still young then and wanted to find something to do. Mrs. Carson was looking for household help, and I jumped at the chance to be with a family." She looked off into the yard. "I've never married. Never had children of my own." She paused, then smiled and looked at me. "There was so much life there with the Carsons. With those three boys. Always something with those three."

"Sounds like you had your hands full. How old were the boys?"

"Jeremiah was only ten when I started. Zachary was seven, and William was four. The judge and his wife kept me on after they'd grown up. Such a lovely couple. So kind. After the boys were gone, the house ran itself, really. I just did some light work for them, tended their dogs while they traveled. I loved my time there. The house and gardens up there are beautiful."

Ah, yes, the good life on the Hill.

Germany and I each took another cookie. A brilliant flash of red caught my eye. A cardinal landed on a flat feeder attached to a post mid-yard. Greta pointed, "Look at that! Isn't he gorgeous?"

We watched the cardinal crack black oil sunflower seeds with his fat beak. "Such beauty," Greta whispered.

The cardinal flew away, and I steered us back to the topic. "When did you stop working for the Carsons?"

"I was almost eighty." She looked up at the umbrella, evidently doing the math. "Fourteen years ago. I'll be ninety-four in December. I bought this little house and have been keeping myself busy ever since."

I steered back to the question at hand. "I wanted to meet you to ask you about something."

She looked at me, expectant. "What's that, dear?"

"I heard through the grapevine that you know a secret about the Carsons."

She took a paper napkin and started rubbing the condensation off her glass of lemonade. "I don't know what you mean. The Carsons are one of the finest families in this town. If they have a secret, I'll take it to my grave."

"So you won't tell me?"

Greta Bullfinch's face went stony. "Nothing to tell. It's been lovely to meet you both," she said as she stood. "But I've got a church committee meeting at Holy Assumption this evening, so we'll have to cut this short."

The teacher, dismissing her students.

Germany and I got back into Cricket.

He said, "That was sure a waste of time."

"Not at all," I said. "Her reaction confirmed that there's a secret. And she said she *will* take it to her grave. There's a secret, all right, and we need to find out what it is."

"Impressive," Germany said, nodding. "Very impressive."

Yep. Smart kid.

CHAPTER TWENTY-SIX

W E LEFT GRETA BULLFINCH, and I noticed a missed call. Unknown number. No message left. Maybe it was Onyx. I called back. Voicemail full. *People! Clear out your voicemails!*

I drove to the address I'd found online for Onyx. No sign of the red Mercedes on the street.

Onyx lived in an enclave of buildings north of town near where the Champlain River joins the Wolf. The apartments were built in the last few years, with color-blocked exteriors in muted red, green, and blue. They have underground parking, a particularly desirable amenity in our winters.

Nice views, small spaces, big rents.

Germany and I went into the three-story building. A security panel with door buzzers was inside the lobby next to the mailboxes. I rang the buzzer for O. Lyden, apartment 222. No answer. I took another one of my cards and wrote my cell number on the back with, "Sorry I missed you. Really need to talk about Maisie." I stuck the card through her mailbox slot.

Anxious whispered, *Isn't it a felony to put things in someone's mailbox other than US mail?* Badass told her to shut up before I could.

We got to Gram's just before six. Nathan, Gram, and my mother were at the dining room table, just starting to dig into the Finnish *gala lohta,* a salmon and potato casserole that's one of Gram's specialties.

Sitting next to my mother? Nick Milcross. He smiled when he saw me, got up, and gave me a hug.

He smelled like sawdust and man. Yum.

He said, "I was doing some finish work in the carriage house, and your grandma invited me for dinner. I hope that's okay with you." He gave me a grin.

I looked at Gram. She winked at me. I turned to Nick. "Oh, gosh, I guess I can tolerate having you here."

Anytime. Anywhere. Lonely Me got excited. *Ooh, do we love Nick?*

Anxious Me whispered a warning. *Too soon. Too soon.*

I introduced Germany to the group, and we sat down, me next to Nick and Germany on my other side.

"I've been to Germany," Nathan said and told us about the trip he and his late wife had taken to Europe. He looked at me, "You remember, don't you, Evelyn?"

Germany looked at me, questioning.

Gram interceded, patting Nathan's arm. "Nathan, dear. That's not Evelyn, that's Mackenzie."

Nathan stared at me with a pained expression.

I felt a tug in my heart. "I wish I *was* Evelyn, Nathan. She made you happy, didn't she?"

Tears formed in his eyes, and his lower lip trembled. "I'm sorry. I get so confused."

Gram grabbed his hand. "It's all right, sweetheart. It's all right." She rose off her chair to hug him. The rest of us concentrated on our plates.

Nathan returned to eating his dinner.

I asked my mother, "How's the job search?"

She smiled, "I have an interview tomorrow." She'd applied at Citizen's Bank in town. "Maybe I'm not as ancient as I thought."

Gram asked Germany about himself, and he willingly supplied details.

"Working for a big-city detective. How exciting!" Gram said.

I felt a prickle of annoyance. Gram had no idea what a you-know-what Sheena Shay was. I wanted to set everyone straight, to tell them how Sheena had been fired from the police department and that she was a manipulating, conniving—

Gram turned to me. "And how nice she's here to help you, dear."

My whole body tensed. Nick must have sensed that. He reached under the table and patted my leg. I met his eyes. His smile was calming, reassuring. I exhaled and relaxed.

Lonely Me whispered, *He's so good for us. We should love him.*

After dinner, Germany offered to help my mother do the dishes. Gram took Nathan upstairs for the night.

Nick and I stepped out the back door. He said, "Let me show you what I did in your place today." He led me by the hand to the carriage house. *We could hold his hand forever,* Lonely said.

The sun was low in the sky, the evening air warm. A soft breeze rustled the leaves of the maples. We stepped into the carriage house, and he turned toward me, wrapped his arms around me, and pulled me into a kiss. A lovely kiss. A warm kiss. A long kiss.

I felt kind of melty inside. *We could do this forever*, Lonely said.

Anxious Me warned again that we were moving too fast. *Danger! Initial stirrings!*

Badass Me suggested we just go right up to the bedroom loft and take care of business.

Anxious Me hesitated. *No, no, no. Too much too soon is not good.*

While they argued, Nick showed me the baseboards and trim he'd finished in the kitchen and living area. Then he walked me back to Gram's.

Germany came outside just then. "Mack, I need to get back to Trip's." He and Sheena were bunking there.

"I can drop you off," Nick said. He tossed Germany the keys to his Land Rover. "I'll be there in a minute."

Germany headed to the car, and Nick hugged me again. Kissed me again and whispered, voice deep and breath warm against my neck, "I'll come back this weekend and help you move in, okay?"

Every part of me wanted the moment to last, to stay right there in his arms forever. Every part of me watched him drive away, wanting more.

When I went back inside, my mother was at her computer at the dining room table. She waved me over. "Look at this, Mackenzie. Tell me what you think."

I stood behind her. She'd created a dating profile on one of the dating websites. "I'm signing up for Mucho Matches. I'm also thinking about joining Best Bet, The Right One, and Happily Ever After.

"Mom! What the heck? Those sites are horrible."

"Well, my friend Doris from the bakery met a man from The City on Mucho Matches. They text and talk every day."

"Has she met him in person?"

"No, but she says she will any day now. He's just been really busy with work."

"'Busy with work' means he's probably married."

She looked at me wide-eyed. "Seriously? Why would he lie?"

I patted her shoulder. "Oh, Mother, Mother, Mother. You have much to learn about today's world. Besides, you have Duncan. Why are you even doing this?"

She huffed as the air quotes flew. "Because I do not 'have' Duncan. Because Duncan decided to 'have' someone else! So why shouldn't I?"

I sat next to her, took her hands in mine, and met her eyes. "Mom. Duncan loves you. This is all just a misunderstanding. And I can guarantee there isn't any other guy on a dating website who is a better match for you than Duncan is."

She pulled her hands away and swiped at her eyes. "Well, until *he* sees that, I'm going to keep looking around."

"Just be careful, okay?"

She waved me away.

There should be a dating website called Last Resort.

CHAPTER TWENTY-SEVEN

Friday, June 28

THE DOOR TO THE middle office was closed when I got to TriMak on Friday morning. I knocked, hoping Germany was there. I liked having him around, liked having him think I was brilliant. What can I say?

After a moment, the door opened. Sheena smiled at me. Wearing a white, silky blouse and navy slacks, she looked polished and professional. *The witch.* The desk behind her held a briefcase, her laptop, and a water bottle. A green sweater was draped over the back of the chair. She was obviously making herself at home. In *my* office.

I asked, "Is Germany around?"

"Nope. I sent him out for supplies."

Errands for her majesty, Queen Sheena. Blecch. A cigarette smoldered in an ashtray on the desk. Stinking up the office. *Mine!*

I wrinkled my nose. "We're non-smoking here," I said.

"Yeah, I'm trying to quit. It's temporary. I'm just a little extra stressed right now."

Maybe because those "bad people" Germany had mentioned were after her?

She went to the desk and crushed the cigarette out, then turned to me. "Say, kiddo, could you get me a cup of coffee? I need a jolt."

Who did she think I was? Not "kiddo." Not Trip's secretary, and certainly not "the girl who fetches coffee."

"We all make our own around here, so help yourself," I said. "Coffee maker's back there." I pointed to the kitchen, turned, and went to my desk.

I heard her in the kitchen, clanking around. After a few minutes, she came out to the front reception area, coffee in hand. She stood at the counter and fixed me with a look. "So let me understand the deal here. You're not Trip's secretary. You're not in charge of coffee. So who are you exactly?"

I explained how I'd have my investigator's license any minute now. How I used to work for Trip. How he'd invited me—begged me, actually—to be part of TriMak. "The agency is named after *me*—after *us*. Trip and Mack. Tri*Mak* Investigations. *That's* who I am."

Snarky whispered, *Tell her to put that in her pipe and smoke it.* I could tell Snarky and Sheena were never going to be buddies.

Sheena gave me an indulgent smile. "I understand now. Didn't mean to step on anybody's toes. No offense." Her voice was syrupy-sweet as she asked, "So what have you got on my Maisie Gordon case?"

"*Your* case?"

"Okay, *our* case. But the dead girl's grandfather hired me *before* the mother hired you, just for the record."

"Um, not true, Sheena. Remember? Mrs. Gordon called her father *after* she hired *me*. Just for the record."

She curled her lip. "Whatever. So, what do you have so far? I'm here to help." Something in her tone suggested she thought we could use all the help we could get.

Ooh! Big-city cop comes to little ol' Three Rivers—beyond Podunk. Swooping in to show us hicks how things are supposed to be done. Well, I understand how things are done in Three Rivers and don't need you getting in my way, thank you very much. Badass was in rare form.

Sheena took a sip of coffee. "So you gonna tell me what you have so far?"

I wasn't in the mood to share. The front door opened, and Germany came in carrying a big box.

Sheena brightened. "There's my right-hand man." She gave me a look. "*He* makes my coffee."

Germany said, "I got the rest of the stuff you wanted." He carried the box to the middle office.

The rest of the stuff? This felt more than temporary.

Sheena read my mind. "This is all short-term, like I said. Just until we resolve the question for the old man. That's all."

She went back to her—*no, my middle*—office. Trip came in through the back door, saw her in there, and went in. A second later, Germany came out, closed the door, and sat by me.

The chief came in from the back and came to the counter by my desk. He wrinkled his nose. "Since when are you a smoker?"

I wrinkled back. "Not me. Her majesty." I gestured in Sheena's direction with my thumb. "She says she's trying to quit."

"You tell her we're non-smoking here?"

I nodded. "Told her. Doesn't seem to care."

"Well, it's a hard habit to break. Any news on the Gordon case?"

I told him about Greta Bullfinch, the "lead" that Gram had given me. "Some kind of secret about the Carsons."

He frowned. "Tread carefully with that, Mackenzie. Rollo Carson is one of my oldest friends and one of the best people in this town."

Trip and Sheena emerged from the middle office and approached us. His hair was mussed. Her blouse was buttoned crooked. Canoodling, indeed.

Trip said, "We're, uh, going to take off for the day."

Sheena leaned into his side, her hand on his back. She slid the hand lower, and he gave a little yelp and jumped. *Geez. A man doing that to a female coworker would earn himself a lawsuit.*

My voice was as firm as I could make it. "Take off. I don't care. I'm not your secretary, Trip!"

His cheeks colored as Sheena wrapped an arm around his waist and steered him toward the back door. Before they got there, Trip made a little mewling sound as Sheena grabbed him and got him in a lip-lock. The kiss lasted. And lasted. And lasted.

We stared until the chief cleared his throat. We all looked away. The chief asked, "So what are you two working on?"

I told him we were tracking down people who knew Maisie Gordon. I heard the back door close. "They're gone. Finally."

The chief blew out a breath. "Good Godfrey, what's their deal? Trip's acting like a fool."

I shook my head. "I don't get it.

"I do," Germany said. "She has that effect on guys."

We both looked at him. "What effect?" I asked.

"They see that she's strong, confident. She can shoot straighter and out-drink any guy. Men get stupid around her. She's a challenge. Wild. They want to tame her. Dominate her."

I looked at the chief. "Is that true for you, Chief?"

He snorted. "Me? Hell no! I don't like her kind of female. I like my women warm and soft—"

"Wait just a sec," I said. "You told me I was too soft and made me go to the gym to get tougher."

"Whoa, Chickie! You're not a woman."

I shot him a look. "Excuse me?"

He laughed. "Well, I mean not in the man-woman sense. Nothing personal. We're colleagues. Coworkers. Fellow members of the Justice League, keeping the world safe for democracy."

I laughed at the image. Trip thinks of the three of us as superheroes too. "Okay, so I assume you're Superman. Then, Trip would be—?"

He thought for a second. "Batman. Rich enough to have a butler."

"And that makes me who?"

He grinned. "Wonder Chickie!"

Germany laughed. "You guys are great. I wish I could work here."

The chief headed to his office. I turned to Germany and asked, "You want to come with me to fight for truth, justice, and the American way? Solve a mystery? Maybe find a parakeet?"

"Sure. Sheena won't miss me."

"Then let's roll," I said, feeling very Wonder Chickie. Yeah. Badass Wonder Chickie.

CHAPTER TWENTY-EIGHT

NEEDED TO TALK TO Jemma Dalworthy Provost again. She was the last person to see Maisie alive, according to the police report.

As we drove south toward Campbell, Germany thanked me again for inviting him to dinner at Gram's. "I like your family. Your mom is nice, but she's, uh, kind of . . ." He paused.

I offered some suggestions. "Angry? Anxious? Pushy? Annoying?"

"Angry, yes. Because she's heartbroken."

I was well aware of how anger covers harder emotions. "Aw, geez, did she tell you about her boyfriend?"

"Oh yeah," Germany said. "All the gory details. Name's Duncan, right?"

"Yep. They broke up this week."

"She said he cheated on her."

"That's what she thinks, but we don't know that for sure.

She might be overreacting. Her anxiety gets in the way some-times. A lot."

He said quietly, "Okinawa is like that." Germany told me how his sister struggled with anxiety and depression. She'd been hospitalized a couple of times for trying to hurt herself.

"I'm so sorry, Germany. Is it hard for you, working on this case with us?"

"I'm fine with it," he said. "It's not about me. But I under-stand how someone can feel so low they want to hurt themselves. I've seen it. But this girl? Maisie? She seemed to be fine. Killing herself doesn't seem to fit."

"Except she left that note." I hesitated, then decided to go for it. "Did your sister leave any notes when she, um, tried to . . . ?" I couldn't find the words.

"Kill herself? No. Never left any notes. Just took pills. Not at all like on TV or in movies. No notes. Just actions."

"So maybe she OD'd by accident?"

"Nope. She told me it was on purpose."

"What was her reason?"

"She wouldn't tell me. I think something happened to her when she was about twelve. She changed about then, started getting moody, depressed."

"Might have been her hormones—starting puberty." I knew all about that. "Or do you think someone was abusing her?"

Germany got quiet, looked out the window. "Possibly. She's never said."

We drove past the city limits into the countryside. Rolling green fields planted with corn, soybeans, and alfalfa spread to the east and west of the highway. Cows and sheep dotted the pastures.

I let the minutes pass, then asked, "How is Okinawa now?"

Germany smiled. "She's great. Married to an army guy. They live in Georgia. They have twin boys."

Whatever storm his sister had gone through, it was over now, evidently. Maisie's storm was over too.

We pulled into the Provost's driveway. The same boy answered the door. Same boy, different tee shirt. GAME ON, it said above a picture of a video game controller.

I smiled. "Hi again. Is your mom home?"

"Nope. She went to the store."

"Your dad here?"

"Nope. He's at work."

I smiled. "I was here the other day. What's your name again? Was it Bruce?"

"Bryce. But everyone calls me Bubba. Actually, I'm Bubba Junior. My dad is Big Bubba. Our babysitter is here." He turned his head and hollered, "Hey, Crystal!"

"Don't bother her," I said. "Tell your mom I stopped by and I'll come back to see her another time."

Driving back to Three Rivers, I told Germany how Jemma had insisted that she had no idea who Maisie's mystery B was. "What if it was her husband? His nickname is Bubba. Maybe Jemma dated him in high school."

Germany ran with it. "And Maisie had a crush on him, and Jemma found out and got mad."

My turn. "And followed her up to the cliff, and they fought."

"They fought, and then—" Germany went silent, staring out the side window. Thinking about his sister, maybe.

"Hey, Germany, we're just spit-ballin' here," I said, trying to lighten the mood. "This is how we figure things out. We imagine possibilities. Sometimes we think maybe one plus one will equal two. But it turns out to be something entirely different. We can't be sure what happened until we know for sure what happened. Meanwhile, it's all just theories. That's how this works."

He said nothing.

"Germany? You okay?"

He shook off whatever had him, looked at me, and smiled. "Yeah, yeah. Fine. It's all just a lot to think about."

We made small talk, mostly about the weather, all the way back to TriMak.

CHAPTER TWENTY-NINE

NOBODY WAS IN THE office when we got back. Germany said he wanted to walk around downtown, maybe check out Java Java and get some food.

I teased him. "Or maybe stop by the yoga studio and check out Tansy?"

He blushed and denied it, a little too vehemently.

After Germany left, I noticed that something was not right on my desk. Somebody had been going through my stuff. Things in the desk drawers were not where I'd left them. Things on the desk had been moved—slightly, but enough that I noticed.

My first thought was that Sheena had been snooping, looking for paper notes, addresses, names, anything that would help her resolve the Gordon case before I could. *Competitive beyotch*, Badass snarled.

Second thought? Maybe it was the chief looking for something. But what? I looked at the desktop again. Something was missing. The yearbook.

My work cell rang. "Tri—" was as far as I got.

Jemma Provost screamed at me. "What the hell were you doing, showing up at my house and giving my son the third degree?"

"Jemma, what are you talking about?"

"I know you were here! Don't lie to me!"

I took a beat, then said, "He's a very nice boy—very polite. You should be proud. But I was there to talk to *you*. You were the last to see Maisie, weren't you?"

"So what? How does that give you permission to harass my kid?"

I ignored the accusation and kept my voice calm. "Jemma, I'd like to talk with you about that night—Maisie's last night. Can we do that?"

She got quiet, then let out a breath, calming a little. "Why talk about that? It's ancient history. And I told the police everything at the time."

"I'd just like to hear about it from you directly. Anything you remember, that's all."

She was silent. I could hear her breathing. I said, "Maisie's mother is dying, and I want to be able to assure her I covered all my bases. You understand?"

She let out a heavy sigh. "Fine. Come on over."

If we ended up talking about her husband, I didn't want anyone overhearing our conversation. "Can we meet somewhere else? Somewhere private?"

"Ugh! Fine. I'll come there later." She was losing patience.

I didn't want her to come to TriMak in case Sheena was around to eavesdrop. "How about Java Java?" I looked at the time. "One o'clock? I'll buy lunch."

"Can't. It'll have to be after four when Steve gets home."

"So dinner then? Say five o'clock at Donatello's? My treat."
I don't know anyone in this area who would turn down a free
meal at Donatello's. Jemma agreed.

Ten minutes later, my personal cell rang. Caller ID showed
that same unknown number from before. I answered.

Onyx Lyden had a pleasant voice. I told her I wanted to talk
with her about Maisie Gordon, how Maisie's mother was dying
and wanted answers.

She oozed compassion. She was probably a great nurse.
"That poor woman. Poor Maisie. Yes, sure. I'll be happy to talk
with you."

I had a brilliant idea. "How about we meet at Donatello's
at five?"

Onyx accepted the invitation. I disconnected and smiled.
Two birds, one stone.

Sheena Shay could bite me.

CHAPTER THIRTY

ID-AFTERNOON, GERMANY AND I were at my desk. I was showing him more of the software we use for investigations. I heard sirens and looked up to see a fire truck and an ambulance in front of the building. We ran outside. Brother Greg came off the truck. "We got a Life Alarm call for this address," he said. "You okay?"

"Yes. It must be Ralph. Upstairs." I pointed at the narrow stairway between TriMak and the shop next door. Greg disappeared up the stairs. Two other EMTs followed with a gurney.

Ralph Quentin is almost eighty and has had some health problems in the past. He rents one of the four apartments above our office from Trip. A couple months back, Ralph had shown me the Life Alarm he wore on a string around his neck. He'd imitated the TV commercials. "If 'I've fallen and I can't get up,' one push of this little button, and help is on the way. Best idea ever!"

I agreed it was a great idea and wondered if Gram had thought about getting one—for Nathan, of course. How insulted Gram would be if I suggested she get one for herself.

I waited in front of the building until they brought Ralph down—strapped to the gurney, oxygen mask on his face. I grabbed his hand and squeezed reassurance as he went by.

The ambulance siren wailed as they headed for Our Lady of Mercy. Greg came down and asked if we had a key to lock Ralph's place. I nodded.

Greg said, "It's like an oven up there. Poor old guy had heat stroke, severe dehydration. Collapsed. Maybe broke something. Lucky he had the sense to push his Life Alarm. That window air conditioner needs to be replaced."

"I'll let Trip know."

Greg said, "The old man asked if you could take care of the dogs. Can you handle it?"

I nodded. Greg gave a wave as the firetruck drove off.

I was sure I could handle feeding and watering Ralph's three dogs—Larry, Moe, and Curly. I was also certain they could *not* be trusted to be cooped up in Ralph's empty apartment while he was away. And especially in this heat.

But what could I do? Gram's Victorian was full, with me, Gram, Nathan, my mother, Chloe the cat, and my parakeets, Tweet and Chirp. No room at the inn. No way I could add three dogs to that mix.

Germany and I went up to Ralph's apartment. Old Larry, the black and tan German shepherd mix, paced the living room. Larry was usually asleep unless Ralph was walking the dogs. This was a lot of excitement for ol' Lar.

Curly, the brown, long-legged, some-kind-of-doodle, was counter-surfing for snacks in the kitchen.

Moe greeted me with wagging, drooling ecstasy and started licking my feet. What can I say? Moe loves me, as in adoration. Worship. Maybe I smell like sausage.

Moe is, according to Ralph, a "shar-pit." A wrinkly blend of shar-pei and pit bull. Ralph told me that some people would call Moe a "pit-pei," but Ralph thinks shar-pit is easier to say. So shar-pit it is.

Germany said, "This is a lot of pooch for a little space."

I agreed. "What am I going to do with you guys?" I asked the dogs. They had no answers for me.

"You can't just leave them here," Germany said.

"True. Left alone, Curly will be gnawing the cupboards. And old Larry is already pacing. Who knows what piles of anxiety that'll create?" I pointed at Moe. "And this one? He loves people. He'll be miserable without human contact."

I made up my mind. "Okay, guys, we're going to have a little adventure for a couple days." I gathered their bowls and toys into a plastic garbage bag. I carried the bag, and Germany carried the big bin of their food down to the office.

We went back up to get the dogs. Larry and Moe were watching as Curly, on top of the dining table, finished off a bowl of butter.

Larry gave me a look that clearly said, "Don't blame me! It's the doodle's fault."

Moe's drooling expression said, without question, "I want some of that!"

We wrangled the three mutts into their leashes and took them—rather, they took us—down the stairs. I wondered how Ralph, at his age, had the strength and balance to walk all three. But he never seemed to have a problem. Good pack leader. I hoped I could fill those shoes.

Germany and I walked Larry, Moe, and Curly around to the back of the building, where they each took advantage of the weeds and dirt to do their business. We went into TriMak through the back door and brought the dogs to the front, where I could keep an eye on them.

"Okay, fellas, you just make yourselves at home here for now. We'll figure out our options later."

Old Larry gave a sigh and stretched out on the floor in the reception area, and within a minute, was snoring. Curly, true to his name, curled up next to him. Germany knelt and started petting them both.

Moe, predictably, settled down on the floor by my desk, head on his crossed paws, in a perfect spot for adoring me.

The chief, Trip, and Sheena came in through the front door. They'd been somewhere all together. I didn't spend a second feeling jealous they hadn't invited me.

Well, maybe a second.

Trip pointed at the dogs. "Explain, please?"

I told them about Ralph and asked how they felt about divvying up the dogs. "Just until Ralph comes home. Couple of days, max."

Chief Bronson looked at Larry snoring on the floor. "Reminds me of one of our K9 officers back in the day. And he looks like he won't be much trouble at my place."

Trip pointed at Moe. "Too much slobber. Besides, he'd be miserable away from you." He pointed at Curly. "And that one is just a giant pain in the ass."

Curly likes to dig holes in the dirt behind our building. Trip had recently stepped in one of those holes and twisted his ankle. Curly became "that damn doodle" from then on. "It can go to the pound for all I care."

That got Curly's attention. He looked up and tilted his head at Trip, eyebrows knit. *Pound? Huh?*

I didn't want to say it, but I did. "Uh, Trip, Ralph had to go to the hospital because the AC up there quit working. You're the landlord. Don't you think you have some responsibility here?"

He sputtered. "Well, I can't be respons—" He stopped to watch Sheena as she knelt down by Curly. She ran her long fingers through his fur. Trip seemed to be fascinated by every move she made. *Ugh.*

Her voice went up an octave. "Trippy, just look at this sweet puppy. Look at his sweetie pie face." Curly rolled on his back, and she rubbed his belly. Sheena crooned, "Good boy. Such a good boy."

Curly was in heaven. "Trippy" seemed to be as well. He'd have been wagging if he had a tail.

I imitated Sheena. "Yeah, Trippy, just look at that sweetie pie face. He promises to be good. Who's a good boy?"

Curly's tail thumped against the floor, and he closed his eyes. Ecstasy.

Germany joined the fun, whining, "Aw, please, Dad. Can't we keep him? I promise to feed him and walk him."

Sheena chimed in with a little girl's voice. "Please, Daddy, please?"

Trip laughed. He'd probably begged his own father just like that. "Fine. Whatever."

Sheena jumped up and kissed Trip on the cheek. "Thanks, Daddy." They made eye contact. Intense eye contact. She put a hand on either side of his face, pulled him in, and kissed him again, on the lips this time.

Ew. Not how you kiss your dad.

Trip blushed. He and Sheena took Curly, some food, and toys and headed out. Trip's new mantra was evidently, "Whatever Sheena wants, Sheena gets." *Sucker.*

The chief left with Larry and supplies.

I looked at Moe. "It's just you and me, kid."

"And me," Germany said.

"And you," I said with a smile.

Germany and I spent the next hour at my desk, talking. At closing time, I put Moe's leash on him. He wagged his whole body, wrinkles rippling, slobber spraying.

Germany asked me to drive him to Trip's. We got into Cricket and I attached Moe's leash to the seatbelt in the back seat. He drooled all over my fake leather upholstery.

I dropped Germany off, and as I drove home, I lowered the back driver's side window. Moe stuck his head out. I glanced in the side mirror. Moe's wrinkles flapped in the breeze, a stream of slobber flying back toward any car unfortunate enough to be following us.

Moe looked like he was smiling. I smiled at him. Jimbo was uncharacteristically silent all the way to Gram's.

I parked behind the Victorian and peeked through the glass in Gram's back door. Nobody in the kitchen. "C'mon Moe. Be quiet."

I stepped into the house, Moe following obediently, just as my mother came into the kitchen from the dining room.

She looked at Moe, then shook her head. "No," she said. "Oh, no. No! Not another animal!" Extra cranky. I couldn't blame her. She'd lost her job and her boyfriend.

"Mom, it's temporary. His owner—"

She cut me off. "No, I don't want to hear the sob story. This place is becoming a zoo! That animal *cannot* stay here."

Gram came into the kitchen. "What animal?" She saw Moe and grinned. "Aw, look at the little wrinkly thing! My goodness, he sure wouldn't win any beauty contests. He is a *he*, isn't he?"

"Yes, and his name is Moe." I explained Ralph's plight. "Moe's brothers Larry and Curly—"

Gram laughed. "The Three Stooges! That's adorable!"

My mother rolled her eyes and gave a grunt of disgust.

I said, "Larry is staying with the chief, and Trip has Curly. Is it okay if Moe stays with us for a couple days, just until his owner comes home?"

Moe gave a little whimper, as if pleading his case. He looked at Gram with his big brown eyes, his wrinkles forming an upside-down letter Y, down his forehead and across his jowls.

"Of course. All lost souls are welcome here." Gram reached down to pat Moe's head, which activated his tail.

My mother gave another grunt. "Dear God, who are you? Mother Teresa? Where is it going to end?" *So dramatic.*

Gram's face set as she shot my mother a look. "It ends when I say it ends. My roof. My rules." That look and those words— familiar to me from childhood—said it all: End of story. No point arguing. *Silence, whippersnapper! The Great and Powerful Gram has spoken.*

My mom went back to setting the dining room table for dinner. She knew when she was beaten.

Dinner that night was going to be pork chops with what Gram calls "milk gravy," mashed potatoes, and cheesy biscuits. Tossed salad with Gram's homemade dressing on the side.

This would be a very hard dinner to pass up, but I had to get to Donatello's.

Gram said she was happy to dog-sit for Moe.

Judging from my mother's grunts and mutterings, she was not.

CHAPTER THIRTY-ONE

DONATELLO'S WAS STARTING TO fill up when I got there at four-forty-five. I asked for a table in a quiet corner and told the hostess I was meeting two friends. She took their names.

Jemma arrived. The hostess pointed to me just as a short woman with wavy red hair, dressed in scrubs, came through the door.

I heard Jemma squeal. "Onyx? Oh my god!" They hugged. The hostess brought them to me.

After introductions, the two of them spent the next ten minutes catching up. I listened in. Onyx never married, loved her job as a nurse. She was tickled pink that Jemma had four children. Yes, she'd love to get together anytime.

Dinner arrived. I ate my fettuccine while they talked on. It wasn't until the meal was done that they seemed to remember I was at the table.

"Oh, gosh," Onyx said. "We've been rude. So sorry. You wanted to talk about Maisie."

"Let's do that over dessert and coffee," I said. They decided to split a piece of turtle cheesecake. I sipped my decaf. "I'd like to hear anything you remember about Maisie," I said and sat back in my chair.

They exchanged a look. Jemma nodded at Onyx, a signal to go first.

Onyx said, "She was such a sweet girl. The three of us were very close." She recounted the fun they had, the sleepovers, hanging out. Jemma added memories of birthday parties and bike rides.

Girls just wanting to have fun, as the song says. Until it's not fun anymore.

I said, "Jemma, you saw her last. Where was that?"

Jemma hesitated and looked at the floor. "Hmm." Another pause. She looked up. "She asked me to give her a ride to Cliffside Park. She was meeting someone there. Wouldn't tell me who it was."

"What time was that?"

"Um, nine? Or ten, maybe?"

"You had a car?"

Jemma said, "Yes, my father got a new car every couple of years. So, we always had one of his older ones to drive."

Onyx piped up. "I had that old Volkswagen. Remember, Jemma?"

Jemma laughed. "Remember when the muffler fell off? It was so loud!"

I steered them back on topic. "Jemma, you saw Maisie last. Was she wearing her birthstone necklace that night? It's very important to her mother that I find it. It wasn't on her when her, uh, body was found."

Jemma closed her eyes for a moment, then looked at me. She nodded. "Yes. I'm sure she was wearing it when I saw her."

"Okay, thanks. It must be on that cliff somewhere, or maybe down in the rocks. I know where to look now. Thanks." I shifted gears. "Any idea who she was meeting? Could it have been the boy she liked? B-something?"

Onyx said, "Maisie never told us who he was." She took a bite of dessert.

Jemma stared at the cheesecake on her fork.

I went for it. "Jemma, did you date your husband in high school?"

She paled, then got angry. "Why the hell would you ask me that? You think he's the one Maisie liked? Just because his nickname is Bubba?"

Interesting reaction. I feigned ignorance. "Oh? Is it?"

Jemma glared at me and shouted, "You know damn well it is. My son told you!"

Customers at other tables looked at us. Onyx squirmed in her chair and looked out Donatello's front window.

I shrugged. "It's just a question. Were you dating in high school?"

Jemma took the cloth napkin from her lap and threw it on the table. "I'm done! You harass my son, and then you accuse my husband—"

I held up my hands. "Whoa, Jemma! Nobody harassed anybody, and I'm not accusing *any*one of *any*thing. It was just a question."

She turned to her old friend. "Great to see you, Onyx. Let's get together again, just the *two* of us." She shot me a look and said, dripping with sarcasm, "Thanks for dinner." She turned and stomped off.

Onyx and I sat in silence. She scraped the last of the turtle cheesecake off the plate and closed her eyes while she ate it. She said nothing until after the waiter brought the check.

The chief had told me that it was helpful at times to just let silence go on. He said that people get uncomfortable with silence and can say interesting things to break it. Onyx did not disappoint.

Voice quiet, Onyx said, "He cheated on her. That's why Jemma got so upset. They dated in high school. We were sophomores, and he was a senior. Big jock. Football player. She was crazy about him. He'd cheat and then beg her to take him back. She kept doing it. On and off. On and off. She stayed with him after high school. She got pregnant during college, so they got married. She lost that baby. She and I lost touch after that, but she and Steve stayed together. I don't know if he's still cheating."

"Onyx, is it possible that Steve was the boy that Maisie had a crush on?"

"I don't know. Maisie never said."

"If Maisie had a crush on Jemma's boyfriend, and if he was the one she was meeting—" I let that hang in the air.

Onyx looked like she wanted to throw up.

I pressed on. "Jemma has a pretty bad temper, doesn't she?"

Onyx gave a little nod. "I feel sick. I think I need to leave." She stood up. "Thank you so much for the dinner. I'm sorry we weren't more help."

I handed her my card. "Please call me if you think of anything else." I said again, "Maisie's mother is not doing well at all. She needs to know for sure what happened to her girl." An appeal to Onyx's compassionate side.

She bit her lower lip as she met my eyes and nodded. "I'll let you know if I remember anything. I promise. Thanks again."

As she turned to leave, I said, "Onyx, just one more question." I call this my Columbo move, and it's one of my best things. "Where did you get your Mercedes?"

Her cheeks reddened, and she stammered. "How . . . ? What . . . ?" Then she smiled. "Oh, right. You're a detective. My grandfather left it to me."

I thanked her again. She left, and I sat finishing my decaf. Nurse Onyx inherited the Mercedes. Not a payoff for her silence. Not a bribe for her cooperation. Just an innocent inheritance.

Onyx was off the hook, but I'd poked something in Jemma Dalworthy Provost. Was it an old scar or a more recent wound?

CHAPTER THIRTY-TWO

I T WAS AFTER NINE on Friday night. I was full of Donatello's fettuccine, and the carb coma was setting in. After my busy week, I looked forward to setting the Gordon case aside for the night and zoning out on Netflix in my PJs. I'd packed most of my stuff, ready to move into the carriage house the next day, provided Nick gave the go-ahead.

I settled on my bed in the Rose Room, Chloe beside me and Moe curled on the rug next to the bed. I was firing up my laptop to stream Netflix when my cell dinged.

A text from Vince. I hadn't heard from him in over two weeks. The text was cryptic.

> Urgent need to talk Old Town Tap PLEASE

I debated. Vince had a lot of nerve assuming that I was free on a Friday night. Assuming I'd jump when he asked me to. Assuming I liked him enough to meet him.

He was right on all counts, of course.

I dressed in jeans and a tee shirt—a perfect shade of blue-violet that brought out the green in my eyes. I ran a brush through my hair, swiped on a little mascara and blush.

Gram was still awake, reading in bed, when I peeked in to tell her I was leaving.

"Is it okay if Moe bunks with you until I get back?"

She said it was fine. I brought Moe into her room, and he immediately jumped up on her bed.

I started to reprimand him, but Gram stopped me. "He'll be fine. It's nice to have a little company." Moe curled up at Gram's feet as Nathan snored in the twin bed next to hers.

Twenty minutes later, I stepped into Old Town Tap, a popular bar/restaurant where you can get a pretty good burger and a decent drink. It's had the same black-and-white checkerboard floor tile since, well, forever. Signs on the walls for beverages, past and present, beg for attention. A lighted sign promotes Hamm's beer. Leinenkugel's sign is neon. Guinness. Bud Light. Rolling Rock. Spotted Cow. Grain Belt. Walter's Beer. Shiner on Tap. Makes a girl thirsty just looking around.

The ceiling is tin-paneled above the bar. Big screens carry football games, and tonight, guys in camo driving ATVs.

Vince was in a back booth, nursing a beer, when I got there. He waved. I joined him and asked the server for a glass of water. I wanted to keep my wits about me. And I had too much going on to risk a hangover in the morning. And this was Vince.

Vince plus alcohol-reduced inhibitions equals danger.

"What's up, Vince?"

He reached across the table and grabbed my hand. "I've missed you, Macaroni." He'd teased me mercilessly when I was young. My name—Mackenzie Annabelle—became Macaroni Banana-belly. I pretended to hate it back then.

"I've missed you too," I said, withdrawing my hand. "How have you been?"

His dark eyes drilled into mine. "Lonely. Very lonely."

Lonely Me felt a pang of sympathy. *Poor Vince.* "That's a shame. How's Lori?" I asked about his ex-wife, just to get that out of the way. I knew she'd moved out of town.

He leaned back in the booth. "She's having a great time. Loves her new job. Met somebody."

"Good for her," I said. *Good for us*, Lonely said.

Vince leaned forward, elbows on the table. He took both my hands in his. "So what's the deal with us, Mackenzie? Are we on or what?"

I leaned in. "You tell me, Vincent."

He gave a half-smile. "I'd like us to be on."

I looked into those dark eyes, wanted to touch his dark, curly hair. Wanted to run my hand across his cheek, feel the stubble. I shook my head to clear the rest of where that impulse was heading. "What does that mean? Us being 'on'?"

"You know, dating? Where we go out together, see movies, have dinner, hang out. Remember dating?"

Nick's face drifted through my mind. I pulled my hands away and leaned back in the booth. "I'm kind of seeing someone."

He sat back. "What? Who? Greg told me you were single."

I backpedaled. "Well, kind of seeing if something might develop with someone, I mean."

He grinned. "So you *are* single. So let's do this. What do you say?"

Nick and I had something, but what was it? Nothing official. Just casual. Actually, mostly business with the remodeling project. He was a sweet guy but hadn't made any moves, really. No, not really. A kiss here and there. That's all.

And Vince was, well, hot. *Hot* hot.

Anxious Me was wary. *Not eager to get hurt again.*

I forced a casual tone, going for the middle ground. "Why not? If you're okay with not being exclusive."

Anxious was shocked. *What woman ever says that?*

Badass countered that. *A woman who wants to stay in control of the situation.*

Vince grinned. "Not being exclusive? Works for me, absolutely. Hey, you hungry? I'm getting a burger. You want one?"

"No, thanks. I just ate. I'm tired. I need to get to bed."

He raised his eyebrows and grinned again. "Want company?" That's Vince.

"No thanks. I don't know you that well."

He laughed. "So you're leaving me to fend for myself?"

I patted his hand. "You're a big boy. I'm sure you'll manage. But you can call me sometime and ask me out officially, okay? But don't take too long. I won't be sitting around waiting."

I slid out of the booth. Vince stood, too, and grabbed me. He whispered into my ear, "You drive me nuts." Before I knew it, he was kissing me. Stirring things up. I kissed him back, then pushed him away. I opened my eyes and looked over his shoulder.

Nick was standing there, looking at us. I recognized his parents behind him.

His expression? Confused and maybe a little disappointed. He said nothing, just turned around and followed his parents out of the restaurant.

I was tempted to run after him and try to explain. But what would I say exactly?

My heart hurt all the way home to Gram's.

CHAPTER THIRTY-THREE

S ATURDAY MORNING. MOVING DAY, at last. The carriage house is a great size—about eighteen hundred square feet of living space on the ground floor and half that in the loft bedroom above. Nick had done a beautiful job fitting a kitchen, dining, and living space on the main floor, along with a roomy bathroom with a soaker tub and separate shower.

I'd ordered a smallish couch from Amazon. I opened the box and pulled out the parts. Cushions, arm rests. Back rest, bottom, legs. And some metal bracing pieces. Quite the project.

Nick arrived, walked in the open door, and looked at the couch parts. "Seems pretty straightforward," he said.

I should not have been surprised to see him. He'd promised to help me, and here he was, regardless of how he might be feeling. A man of his word.

Anxious Me asked, *Can we say the same about Vince?*

"Thanks for coming, Nick." I searched his face for signs of hurt or anger. His expression was neutral, as was his tone.

"I said I'd be here, so here I am." He pointed to the parts on the floor. "All you need is a screwdriver and an Allen wrench, and they supply both. Easy peasy."

I took his word for it. Together, we assembled the couch—less than twenty minutes total. I sat and leaned back. "Wow. That was a lot simpler than I expected."

He sat next to me. "Like I said, pretty straightforward."

I looked at him. "Um, do you want to talk about last night?"

He avoided my eyes. "What's to talk about?"

"Well, you saw me with another guy."

He looked at the floor. "You can kiss anyone you want." He cleared his throat and stood. "I'll do the bookshelves next."

We worked together for the next couple of hours. Nick put together two bookshelves and a rolling cart for the kitchen. I set up the coffee maker and made a pot of vanilla hazelnut. While it brewed, I washed and dried my new cups, glasses, plates, and bowls. I lined the cupboard shelves with peel-and-stick paper in a gray-and-white diamond pattern. Little-Bit-of-OCD Me loves a project like that—measuring and cutting, making it all fit just perfectly.

Nick came to stand beside me and said, "Don't know why you need that."

"You mean lining the cupboard shelves?"

"Yeah. What's the point?"

What *was* the point? Lining the kitchen shelves and drawers is just what my mother and Gram have always done. "I don't know. It just looks pretty, I guess."

"So do you," he said, his voice soft.

I turned toward him and brushed my hair off my forehead. "Yeah, I'm sure I do, all sweaty."

He tucked a stray hair behind my ear, then kissed me.

157

"Nick—" I said, hands against his chest.

"Don't talk." He kissed me again.

I pushed him away. "What's going on?"

He stepped back, holding me by my upper arms, gave me a gentle shake. "I like you, Mackenzie. I *like* you. Can't you see that?"

My cheeks got warm. "I like you, too, Nick."

He let me go. "Then what was that last night?"

"He's an old friend. And *he* kissed *me*, just to be clear. He wanted to know if I was interested in dating him."

"Are you?"

I looked at the floor. "I . . . maybe . . . I don't know."

He let me go. "Message received." He headed for the door.

Something told me that if I let him walk out, we'd be done. Not that we'd gotten started. "Nick, wait."

He turned.

Now what? I wanted him to stay, to talk things out. I wanted to be sure he was okay. "I, uh, still need your help."

He looked around. "Looks like you're pretty settled in here."

"No, I need your help upstairs. With the bed."

He paused, frowned. "What?"

Anxious Me freaked out. *Idiot. That sounded like an invitation. Too soon to do the deed!*

I blushed and stammered, "Uh, I mean, uh, the loft isn't anywhere near ready." The loft was full of boxes waiting to be unpacked. My new mattress—one of those foam jobs squeezed into a tiny package—wasn't ready. "I don't even have anywhere to sleep. The mattress is still poofing."

"Poofing? Is that the technical term?" He laughed. *We like his laugh.*

"What would you call it? Uncompacting? Decompressing?"

He laughed again. "Poofing is good, actually," he said. "But you don't really need my help up there, do you? Nothing to assemble, right?"

I shook my head. "You're right. Just boxes to unpack. I can handle it. Can we at least have a donut? A reward for all this hard work?"

We sat at the dining table with coffee and a box of Kwik Stop vanilla crème donuts. The room got warmer by the minute as the heat of the day rose.

I aimed a box fan in our direction. The central air conditioning for the carriage house was installed out back, but when I'd turned it on, I got nothing. I fanned myself with my hands. "Geez, it's hot in here."

"Sorry about that," Nick said. "I'll get our HVAC guy out here on Monday."

We had our coffee and donuts, chatting about nothing in particular, and then Nick had to leave. He was meeting his dad and his grandfather for a planning session. The three of them run Milcross Builders. Kind of a "Three Men and a Hammer" business arrangement. They'd make a great home reno series on HGTV.

At the door, Nick met my eyes. "So? Are you going to go out with him?"

I hesitated. My stomach tightened. Anxious Me was in the house.

Nick spoke, his voice soft. "Don't answer that." He met my eyes. "Like I said, I really like you. Is it okay if I call you? Go out officially? I just, um, well . . ." His turn to blush.

Blushing. Tongue-tied. I like that in a man.

"Yes, Nick. You can call me, and we can go out. Officially."

He grinned. "Great!" He kissed me quickly and smiled again. "That's great! See ya!"

After he left, I looked around the main floor. Nick and I had made good progress. I went into the bathroom and hung up my new towels, thinking about Nick. And Vince. And what I'd gotten myself into. First, no guys, and now two guys? What the heck was I doing?

Anxious Me started spinning worst-case scenarios. Sitcom stuff. Rom-com stuff. Ridiculous stuff.

Rational Me took a breath. *Just wait and see. Wait and see.*

I headed up the stairs to the loft, to my sumptuous bedroom suite, with its half bath for nighttime convenience and a reading nook in the corner.

The mattress was ready. I looked at it and said, "You're poofed!" I thought of Nick and smiled. I wrestled the mattress onto the queen-size bedframe. Sweat stung my eyes.

Note to self: next time, let the mattress poof *on* the frame.

I made the bed with my new bedding from Target—crisp white sheets, a soft white cotton blanket, and a duvet in a soft gray-and-white print. I fluffed my new pillows into place. Four in total, two for me and two for someone else. *Who?*

I unpacked the boxes, put my new bedside lamps in place on the end tables, my clothes into the wide closet on the far side of the loft, and bathroom things in the cabinets.

I screwed the legs into my new, white-and-gray overstuffed chair and angled it into the corner, next to the little side table and antique floor lamp Gram had given me. My reading nook was ready.

I settled into the chair and looked out the wide windows across from the foot of the bed. The windows were open, and a warm breeze moved through the leaves of the maple trees outside.

These maples turn a brilliant yellow in autumn. Gram calls this her "maple cathedral." When we were young, Gram would take us grandchildren outside to stand under the trees in the fall. "Let's be silent. Look up," she'd say.

Silently, we watched the sunlight playing through the golden leaves.

"See what God has done," she'd whisper in awe. Worshipfully. A cathedral, indeed.

I closed my eyes and drifted off.

CHAPTER THIRTY-FOUR

NAPPED IN THE CHAIR until my cell dinged a half hour later. A text from Germany. I called him. "What's up, Germ?"

"Just wondering what you're doing today. Sheena went out with Trip on his boat. Wanna hang out?"

It was hotter than hades in the carriage house loft. "Meet me at the office," I said.

I took Moe with me. His jowls flapped in the wind, the picture of doggie nirvana, as I drove to TriMak.

A block from the office, Charity Gordon called my cell. "My mother isn't doing well. She's back in the hospital. She might not make it to Monday. She keeps talking about Maisie's necklace. She demanded that I call you. It's the drugs making her loopy. Do you have any updates?"

I had zip, so I lied. "Tell her I'm very close to a resolution, and I think I know where the necklace is. I'm going back to the cliff later. Tell her to hang on."

Charity thanked me and disconnected.

I had an idea. I called my brother Greg, and ten minutes later, I picked up his metal detector. He and his children love finding treasures with it. Maybe I'd find the treasure Mrs. Gordon was seeking. If I was lucky.

Greg said his kids would be thrilled to hang out with Moe for a couple hours.

Germany was waiting on the back steps when I got to Tri-Mak. "Why didn't you wait in the car?" I pointed at Sheena's old pea-green Chevy station wagon.

Ha! Miss big-city detective drives an old beater? How successful is she, really? Snarky wanted to know.

Germany said, "The air conditioning is shot. Cooler out here."

No wonder Sheena liked Trip's BMW.

I grabbed two bottles of water from the office fridge, and we headed to the cliff. As we drove, I shared my thoughts about Maisie.

Germany asked, "So you think the necklace might be in the rocks where she fell?"

"Possibly, but I want to check the cliff top first."

The hike up to the top was even more exhausting than it had been the last time. The heat index was high, with a "feels-like" temperature close to one hundred degrees. The metal detector felt heavier by the minute.

Germany stopped halfway up the trail, leaned against the railing, and drank half his water. "Maybe we should come back later. Might be cooler then."

"Mrs. Gordon doesn't have time for that. Wait here or go back to the car if you want, but I'm going up."

He sighed and then followed me, muttering under his breath. I thought I heard him say something rude about Wonder Chickie.

We got to the top and both sat on the guard rail to catch our breath. It was a huge relief to set the metal detector down. We drained our waters, and I tossed the empties into the blue recycle bin at the top of the trail.

After a couple minutes, I said, "The sooner we get this done, the better." I stood and swept the metal detector over the rocks on the cliff's edge. Nothing. No beeps. I continued moving in slow arcs, walking backward from the rocks to the sandy soil.

Beep. Germany used the garden spade I'd borrowed from Greg and unearthed a bottle cap.

Beep. Beep. Three more bottle caps and two metal screws.

Beep. Beep. Beep. A spoon. A fork. And a short metal pipe.

No necklaces.

Germany took a turn, covering the same ground I'd scanned. Nothing new.

I said, "If the necklace is up here, it might be buried really deep. Too deep to detect after all these years."

I looked out toward the river. "Let's say the girl is there." I pointed toward the cliff edge. "Someone grabs her. They fight. The necklace is ripped off. It goes flying." I moved my hands in a high arc, pointed toward the buckthorn bushes near the edge of the cliff to our left. "We need to scan those bushes."

Fifteen minutes later, we'd scanned as far as we could into the thicket. Nothing.

I said, "Dead end. These bushes were probably nowhere near this big when Maisie was up here. Impossible to get through them now."

Germany shrugged. "Now what?"

I pointed to the edge of the cliff. "We go down there and scan the rocks," I said.

We headed down the steep, narrow trail to the river. We slid down the sandy spots. I slipped and landed hard on a rock. Germany pulled me to my feet. I returned the favor when he fell. We eased our way past boulders in the path, taking turns holding the metal detector. We finally reached the riverbank.

"Got to be an easier way to get down here," Germany said.

I pointed east. "There's another easier path, but it's about a quarter mile that-a-way."

"Might be worth going that-a-way when we're done."

"Wimp," I said with a smile.

"Crazy," he said, smiling back.

"Wonder Chickie," I said.

"And I'm your sidekick. What should I call myself?"

We discussed options while I scanned the rocks. "What goes with chicken?" I asked.

"Mashed potatoes. Ooh. I could be Spud."

"Roosters go with chickens."

Germany brightened. "That cartoon rooster. Foghorn something. That could be me!"

"Foghorn is a great sidekick name," I said.

The metal detector started making a lot of noise. I peered down between two boulders. "Something is down there, but I can't see it." I aimed my cell phone flashlight into the crevice. Something sparkled. "Looks like metal. I need something to grab it with. I'm going to have to come back."

We walked the quarter mile to the gentler trail, then hiked back to Cricket. With cold air on high, we headed back to TriMak.

Trip's BMW was there. We went in, and Sheena yelled at Germany again. "You're supposed to be here with me, not running around with—"

My blood pressure shot up. "Sheena, stop! I asked Germany to help me out. Don't yell at him. Yell at me!"

Trip came out of the bathroom at the end of the hall. "What's going on?'

Sheena turned all sweet and sugary. "Nothing, hon." She pulled Germany into the—*my!*—office and shut the door.

Trip looked at me. "What was that about?"

I considered. Did I want to be honest, burst his little bubble? Or pretend Sheena was wonderful? I opted for bubble bursting. "Trip, you don't see it, but Sheena is, uh, not the nicest person."

He frowned. "What are you talking about? She's great. She's got so much experience, real street smarts. We need that around here."

My turn to frown. "We need street smarts? In Three Rivers? Seriously? She comes in here all big-city to show us how it's done. From what I can see, I'm the one doing all the work on the Gordon case while the two of you are off on your boat or wherever, doing whatever it is you're doing."

"She's been working the case."

I leaned back, raised my brows. "*Really?* What *exactly* has she done?"

"She, uh, found the girl's friends, and uh, an old lady who is connected to the Carson family. And the cop who was on the case."

I fumed. "Those are *my* leads, *my* connections. Not hers! She's been snooping in my desk and probably following me!"

"You just don't like her, do you?"

I sighed. "It's not about liking or not liking her, Trip. She's a distraction. A disruption. The chief doesn't—"

"What? What's the chief got to do with this?"

"He doesn't like her."

Trip's face fell. "What? Why not?"

I felt bad. What right did I or the chief have to tell Trip who he could date? I'd hate it if the two of them were judging me. I backpedaled. "It's just that she's, well, kind of abrasive. Hard. He said she's not his kind of woman."

Trip scowled and huffed. "Well, it's a damn good thing he's not the one with her then, isn't it!" He stormed out the back door.

I heard the BMW roar to life and its tires grinding gravel. Fast.

CHAPTER THIRTY-FIVE

IT WAS RAINING BUCKETS. Cats and dogs. Pitchforks and hammer handles. Or, as Gram jokes, "pitchforks and hamburgers." No way I was going back to the rocks to look for Maisie's necklace.

I called Greg. He said they were having a ball with Moe, and he'd be happy to keep him for a couple more hours.

Sheena had left for parts unknown. I assumed she and Trip had more canoodling, or whatever, to do. I was glad to stay at TriMak in the AC. Germany opted to stay with me.

"Great," I said. "I can use your help tracking down these boys from Maisie's class. Can't believe how many B boys there are."

"Checking the girls too?" Germany asked.

"No. Her friends are sure it was a boy she had a crush on. We'll start there." We sat at my desk. I opened my laptop and brought up the list I'd made from the yearbook. "This is what I have so far—twenty-seven possibilities. By the way, I had the yearbook here on my desk. Have you seen it?"

"Yeah, it's on Sheena's desk. I'll go get it."

Grr. My *desk! In* my *office.* Rational Me suggested I get over it. *You'll have that office in due time. No worries.*

And once we fumigate it . . . Snarky has a nasty streak.

Germany came back, yearbook in hand. "These notes were inside it."

My notes for the case, jotted on whatever scrap of paper I could find at the moment. Jemma's address. Notes about Onyx working at the hospital. Gram's note with Greta Bullfinch's contact info. Notes I'd scribbled after our meeting at Greta's house.

Trip had just insisted that she was working the case on her own. *Ha!*

I slammed my hand on the desk and spewed. "These are *my* leads! *My* notes! Sheena had no right to go through my stuff!"

Germany was silent.

I turned on him. "What? You think this is okay?"

His cheeks got red. "I, uh, I'm the one who took that and gave it to Sheena. She said you'd be okay with it. I thought you were."

My throat tightened. "I am completely, totally, one hundred percent *not* okay with it." I got more revved up with every word. "It's an invasion of my privacy. Overstepping the boundaries. She's a controlling, nosy b—" I stopped.

Germany looked ready to cry.

Geez, lighten up. No need to take it out on the kid. I inhaled, counting to four, held it, willing myself to calm down. I exhaled as I counted to six. Calmer, I said, "It's okay. You didn't know."

Germany looked relieved. "I *didn't* know. I'm really sorry."

I smiled. "It's okay, Foghorn."

We got to work on the list. He brought his laptop in from my—the *other*—office, and we searched for current contact information for each B boy. An hour later, we'd tracked down and eliminated seven possible love interests of Maisie's. Six of them had no idea what we were talking about. The seventh had died.

Germany sat back in his chair and sighed. "Twenty left. This is going to take forever."

I smiled. "This is the grunt work of this job. Ninety percent boring."

"The other ten percent?"

"Satisfying, or terrifying, depending on the day." I checked the time. Almost five. "Enough for today. I'm starving. Are you hungry?"

We locked up the office and dodged buckets as we ran to Cricket. Jimbo seemed to love the rain and chirped all the way to Old Town Tap.

The joint was jumping on this rainy Saturday. Every stool along the bar was occupied. Germany and I snagged a booth along the back wall and each ordered a Tap Burger and fries. Germany opted for Mountain Dew, and I ordered a Diet Coke.

Under other circumstances, I would have had a glass of wine—or two. Or three. But there was something about having this twenty-two-year-old admiring me that made me want to set a good example.

I've had times in the past when I've had more to drink than was wise. Times when I wasn't completely present in situations. After my divorce, I soothed my aching heart with wine. Lots of wine. Every night. My therapist at the time, Doctor Angela, suggested I go to AA.

I went to one meeting. I told myself I wasn't like those AA people—they had *real* problems. I never went back.

I think about quitting drinking, but there are just times when I want it. Not that I need it. If I *needed* it, then I'd have a problem. But I can take it or leave it. Today, I left it.

Our food arrived, and I regaled Germany—at his request—with more stories of my adventures as an almost-official investigator. Our meal demolished, our glasses drained, we left the booth. Germany went to the men's room, and I took the check up front to pay.

Someone leaned in from behind and whispered, "Hey, gorgeous."

I caught a whiff of booze, then turned to face Vince.

He slurred slightly. "Who's that you're with? Is that the other guy? Kinda young, isn't he?"

I didn't owe Vince any explanations, especially drunk Vince. "None of your business."

"Aw, Macaroni. I thought we had something going on." He grabbed my arm.

"Um, let go of me, please, Vince. Nothing is going on with him, or with *us* if you don't let me go."

Vince let go. Germany arrived and stood next to me. I made introductions.

Vince eyed him and then leaned into Germany's face. Menacing. "Hands off my girl. You under*shtand*?"

Germany stepped back and raised his hands in surrender. "Don't know what you're talking about, dude."

I pushed Vince away from Germany. "We're working together. Leave him alone."

Vince raised a hand. "Okay, okay. I'm leaving." He pointed at me and winked. "I'll call you," he said and staggered toward the back of the bar.

Oh yes, please do, Snarky said. She would have plenty to say to Vince about this display of what? Territorial dominance? Machismo? *Ugh.* Vince was one guy sober and someone else entirely when he drank. That could complicate things.

When I was married to Billy, we both drank. A lot. And he cheated. A lot. And we fought. A lot. Yes, drinking definitely complicates things.

The rain had slowed as Germany and I picked Moe up from my brother's house. The rain stopped by the time I dropped Germany at Trip's. He told me he was using the guest room and that Sheena was where you'd expect her to be. *All cozy with Trip. He's an idiot if he can't see her for who she is.*

I got to the carriage house, took a shower, and put on my lightest cotton pajamas. Chloe ran ahead of Moe and me as we headed upstairs. I opened the double window in the loft and positioned a fan in front of the windows.

I gave a sigh and sunk into the soft foam of my newly poofed mattress. Chloe took her spot on the other side of the bed. Moe settled on the rug next to me.

Not lonely now, Rational Me said.

A cat and a dog? Not exactly what we had in mind, Lonely Me argued.

I thought about Maisie's mother. How pale she'd looked, her body weakened by the cancer. I thought about Charity, a doctor now, and how helpless she must feel with her mother dying.

I thought about Jemma and her cheating boyfriend, now her husband. I thought about my mother losing Duncan and her job. She deserved a break.

I thought about Sheena and Trip. *Ugh.* But what a nice young man Germany was. "Foghorn." I smiled.

I thought about Vince. What was that display at Old Town Tap? Alcohol-induced stupidity, no question. I was pretty sure Nick would never do anything like that.

I smiled, thinking about Nick. *He makes us smile,* Lonely whispered.

I listened to the remaining raindrops tap-tapping as they fell through the maple leaves. I felt the stirring of a cool post-storm breeze.

An owl hooted somewhere out there in the night. I listened for an answering call. None came. He hooted again.

Loneliest sound in the world.

CHAPTER THIRTY-SIX

Sunday, June 30

SUNDAY PROMISED ANOTHER HOT, humid day after the rain. Gram and Nathan left for the early service at Our Savior's Lutheran.

With no air conditioning in the carriage house until Monday, and the Victorian hotter than blazes, the coolest place for me was the office.

I buckled Moe in the back seat and headed to TriMak to continue my search for the mysterious B boy. Why did it matter who he was? He could just have been some random kid Maisie liked.

But something—call it intuition, or Spidey sense—told me it was important to figure out who he was. As important as finding Maisie's necklace before her mother died. That created a sense of urgency in the case. *No time to take a day off. Keep working.*

I moved the office thermostat from "weekend" to "cool." I made a cup of donut shop coffee, sat at my desk, and opened the yearbook. I wanted to be sure I'd gotten all the possible B boys on my list.

I went through the book again, page by page. Sophomores, juniors, seniors. Homerooms, clubs, sports teams.

The back door opened and closed, and a few seconds later, Sheena slammed her hands on the counter in front of my desk and screamed at me. "You've got a helluva nerve!"

I met her eyes, maintaining a calm demeanor, even as my heart thumped. "Whatever do you mean, Ms. Shay?"

She glared. "You know damn well what I mean! You have no business undermining my relationship with Trip. You've been jealous of me from the minute I walked into this god-forsaken town. And now you're trying to turn him against me. Butt! Out!"

I stood and leaned my hands on my desk. As close as I wanted to get to an angry Sheena. She might decide to toss me through our front window. I hissed, "Now you listen up, madam. You don't start yelling at me and accusing me of stuff! Trip and I go way back, and we have a special bond—"

She gave a snort. "What bond do you two have? He's the boss, and you're just the—" She stopped. A slight smile played on her lips as she raised an eyebrow. "Wait. Don't tell me you two . . . ?" She wiggled her fingers.

My turn to scoff. "No way! We're strictly business. And he's not my boss. We're partners. Trip, the chief, and me. *Partners.* But we are also friends. We watch out for each other, and I just don't want Trip to get hurt."

She leaned in. "Well, here's a news flash for you. He's a big boy. Doesn't need a mommy to protect him."

I screwed up my face. "And he doesn't need some big-city detective wanna-be breaking his heart! You're going to fool around, and then you're going to go back to wherever the hell you came from, and I'm going to be here picking up the pieces."

She stared at me for a second and then looked up at the ceiling. She took a deep breath, let it out, and looked at me. When she spoke again, her voice was softer. "Listen, Mackenzie. I have no intention of hurting Trip. And I totally get how protective you are. I'm the same way with people I care about. So I'm asking you to trust me, I guess, and to trust him. Trip and I know what this is—this whatever we have going on. And, for now, it's great. We don't care about the future. We're just enjoying this. So could you please give us a little space? Reserve judgment? Please?"

I sat back down and sighed. Could I? I didn't trust Sheena, and Trip could be a real doofus sometimes. But could I just let them do whatever it was they were doing?

Badass didn't think so, but Rational Me stepped in. *Let them be. Not your affair. Literally.* I thought about my grandmother butting into my business and my mother giving me unsolicited advice all the time. I hated that.

"Okay," I said at last. "Do your thing."

Sheena smiled, triumphant. "Thanks." She walked away.

Badass whispered, *If she hurts him, we'll have to do something about that.* I pictured Sheena sailing through the front window.

Lonely Me suggested I was jealous of anyone who had romance in their life. Lonely Me wanted to call Nick or Vince, or maybe both, and get something—anything—going. I was going to have to give that some long, hard thought.

I went back to the yearbook. Something rolled around in my mind. Something I'd heard or seen. What was it? This happens when I'm in the middle of solving a puzzle. There are pieces that sort of float through my brain, unconnected bits of information that are there but have no meaning until the moment when things click. I can't explain it. It just happens that way.

I closed my eyes. I waited. And suddenly, there it was.

I needed to talk to Greta Bullfinch again.

It was Sunday morning, and I was pretty sure I knew where to find her. Google told me that Sunday Mass at Holy Assumption would be done at noon. I headed in that direction, parked Cricket on a side street, and waited on the curb outside the church.

Greta Bullfinch came out the side door, put her sun hat on, and started walking in the direction of her house.

"Miss Bullfinch!" I hollered as I trotted after her.

She turned, gave a smile of recognition, and waited.

I caught my breath, then said, "Do you have a moment?"

"Certainly, dear." She smiled again.

I opted for a roundabout approach, hoping to persuade her to share whatever she knew. "I'm wondering if maybe you could help us—" I said, easing my way to the questions I really wanted to ask. Slowly, gently.

Suddenly, Sheena was at my elbow.

I whispered at her. "You followed me? What the heck are you doing?"

She whispered back. "You need my help, so shut up."

"You shut up!"

"No, you!"

Miss Bullfinch cleared her throat. "That is enough!"

We stopped.

In her teacher voice, Greta said, "Did you girls have something for me? Otherwise, I have to get home and tend to my potato salad."

I started again. "Thanks for your patience, Miss Bullfinch. I'm wondering if you could maybe—"

Sheena cut me off with a snort. "Prentice! For the love of God! Quit pussyfooting around!" She turned to the old woman. "Greta! Is William Carson—the boy you called Buddy—the boy Maisie Gordon had a crush on?"

Greta's face turned to stone. "I've told you before, I will not discuss my former employer or his family!" She straightened up and started to walk away.

"Nicely done, Shay!" I shoved Sheena to the side and walked after Greta. She was fast for an old lady. "Miss Bullfinch, you are the only one who can help me get to the bottom of this."

She stopped and turned, fire in her eyes. "There is no *this* to get to the bottom of! The Carsons are wonderful! Pillars of the community! Fine, upstanding citizens!"

"I know that," I said, "but even the best of families—"

She held up a hand. "Stop! I will not discuss this. If you continue to harass me, I will have no choice but to call the police." She turned and walked away.

I let her go. I didn't want to be arrested for assaulting an old woman. Sheena was another story. I turned on her. "Way to screw things up!"

She got huffy. "Well, things weren't going anywhere the way you were doing it!"

I stomped to Cricket, started the engine, and put the air on "max cool." Jimbo chirped a hello.

"What the hell was that, Jimbo? Why'd she have to stick her big nose into things?"

I took off. Sheena pulled in behind me in Trip's BMW. *Now what? Was she going to follow me everywhere?*

At the red light on the corner of Fifth and Elm, near the cemetery, the street widens to four lanes. Sheena and I ended up side by side.

I looked over at her, resisted sticking out my tongue. She shot me a cocky smile, raised her eyebrows, and stepped on the gas.

A vroom of challenge to me.

I sneered and shook my head. *Seriously?* Snarky said. *Are we in high school? You want to drag?*

She vroomed again. Twice.

I rolled my eyes.

The light changed.

She smirked and took off fast, to the west on Elm.

I stayed there a moment, then put on my blinker and took my time turning right onto Fifth toward home.

Geez, grow up Sheena.

Greta Bullfinch was a dead end. This whole case was a dead end. Sheena wasn't helping. She was getting in my way. Whoever had answers wasn't talking, and I was running out of time.

So was Maisie's mother.

CHAPTER THIRTY-SEVEN

A BLOCK FROM GRAM'S, I got a call from Lou. "Are you up for a Sunday drive?" She wanted to take the urn to Stone Creek and "release the ashes," she said.

The Gordon case was at a dead end. Sometimes, taking a little break helps me to figure things out. Like when you fall asleep with a question in your mind, and you wake up with the answer.

I texted Germany, and he jumped at the chance to get away from Sheena and Trip. Poor kid.

I drove, and Lou and I chatted in the front seat on the half-hour drive north while Germany enjoyed the scenery from the backseat. The highway north to Stone Creek runs along the Nicollet River. The Nicollet flows south into the Wolf River in downtown Three Rivers. The Champlain River flows into the Wolf from the northeast. Hence our town's name.

High bluffs rise above the water on the eastern shore of the Nicollet. Germany said, "Those cliffs are amazing. Do people do any climbing around here?"

Lou filled him in on local history as we drove. She's lived here for decades.

We got to Stone Creek, and I pulled into a lovely little spot off the highway on the river. "How's this, Lou?" I asked.

Lou considered. "If we dump the ashes here, they'll just float back down to Three Rivers, won't they?"

"Good point." We found a better spot in a stand of pine trees down a path from a little rest stop with two picnic tables and an iron barbecue grill on a post. A couple sat at one of the tables, playing cribbage.

We walked far enough down the path to be out of sight of the tables. Lou opened the urn. "Dear person, whoever you were, we hope you will find peace here." She tipped the urn. The breeze caught the ashes and carried them off into the trees. Gritty sand poured out of the urn next and then several clumps of something landed on the dry pine needles on the ground.

Bones? Body parts? I didn't want to look.

We looked at each other. We looked down.

Germany said, "Whoa! It's money!" Five rolled-up bundles of bills lay on the ground, each maybe two inches in diameter, wrapped tightly with rubber bands. "Score!" he said, pumping a fist.

"Good heavens," Lou said.

I picked up one of the rolls, brushed the dust off, and unwrapped it. Hundred-dollar bills. Lots of them.

Lou picked up another, riffled through it. "They are all hundreds. Dear Lord, whose money is this?"

I laughed. "It's yours, Lou."

"No. No way. I'm sure I have to turn this in."

"And I'm sure you don't. You bought the abandoned property in the storage unit. This money belongs to you, fair and square."

I said that with a certainty I didn't feel, but the chief would surely know.

We put the cash in the empty urn and drove back to Three Rivers. I asked, "What do you think? Where's the money from?"

Germany suggested it was profit from selling drugs.

Lou doubted that. "I think it's just the money he got from selling his mother's stuff."

I said, "Why hide it in an urn? With ashes? And we still don't know whose ashes those were."

The three of us spun out several more ridiculous scenarios, laughing all the way back to town.

Lou offered to buy lunch. I declined. Germany accepted. He wanted to hear more about Three Rivers. Lou said she'd take him to Trip's later.

I wanted to get home and talk to nobody, do nothing, and forget about other people's problems for a while.

CHAPTER THIRTY-EIGHT

LATE SUNDAY AFTERNOON, I was on Gram's couch in front of the fan, reading the Sunday comics in *The Bull*. Moe was snoozing on the couch next to me. Gram, Nathan, and my mom were all napping upstairs.

Gram is one of the only people I know who subscribes to an actual newspaper these days. When I asked her why she doesn't just read the paper online, she said she'd never do that. She said, "I remember my parents reading the paper. They did the crossword puzzle together."

Honestly, I enjoy reading the actual paper and doing the puzzles too. And maybe someday, I'll have a partner to do the crossword with me. A girl can dream.

Gram's front doorbell rang. I answered.

Duncan stood there, looking awful. "Is your mother here?"

"She's upstairs sleeping. And I'm not sure she's ready to see you." I invited him in, and we sat at the dining room table.

"How is Barbara?" he asked.

I hesitated. What would my mother want me to say? *She's fine and moving on.* What would Duncan want to hear? *She's miserable and wants you back.*

I opted for somewhere in between. "Okay, I guess. What happened with you two?"

He leaned back in his chair, crossed his arms. "She freaked out about something completely innocent."

"She said you were texting some other woman. Is that true?"

"Yeah, but it was innocent. Nothing at all."

"It was something to her." I leaned forward and crossed the mind-your-own-business line. "Are you still in touch with this other woman?"

"No. Absolutely not, as soon as I realized how your mother felt about it." He hung his head. "I know I hurt her. I feel awful about that." He looked up, completely miserable. "Can you persuade your mother to talk to me? She has me blocked everywhere."

"I'm not sure I can do that. She's pretty angry. You know how she gets."

He nodded. "Yeah, I do. Could you at least give her this?" He pulled an envelope from his shirt pocket.

I promised I would, and Duncan left. I took the stairs two at a time and rapped on my mother's bedroom door, then went in. She was sitting up in bed with the fan going and had dozed off with one of her sudoku puzzle books in her lap.

I shook her awake, handed her the envelope, and said nothing.

She looked at it and evidently recognized Duncan's handwriting. She looked at me, tears welling. "Is he still here?"

"Nope, but he asked me to give you that."

Her hands shaking, she opened the envelope. I left her to it, closing the door behind me. Gram and I might not need to have "a talk" with Duncan after all. One could hope.

I went back to the newspaper, ready to work the puzzles. I didn't dare touch the Sunday *New York Times* crossword in *The Bull*—that's Gram's holy grail. An hour later, I'd finished the Wonder Word puzzle, the Jumble, and one of those "how many smaller words can you make from this big word" puzzles. I made twenty-four words and felt proud until I saw that the puzzle maker made thirty-seven.

Wow. You're a genius, Snarky said. I told her to shut up.

The doorbell rang again. My mother came flying down the stairs. "That's for me!"

She opened the door and practically leaped into Duncan's arms, crying. The two of them hugged for an eternity, then drove off in his car.

All was forgiven, obviously. Duncan's note—whatever it said—had worked its magic. Love had triumphed.

That gave me hope that one day, maybe, love would triumph for me too.

So sad that love hadn't triumphed for Maisie Gordon.

CHAPTER THIRTY-NINE

Monday, July 1

MONDAY OFFERED UP A pleasant morning. Gram and Nathan were in the kitchen when I got downstairs.

Gram smiled. "Happy Forchuly week!" This is a family thing. Gram's Finnish grandfather emigrated to America with his wife in the early 1900s. He loved the Fourth of July, which he called, in his broken English, "Forchuly."

Gram is unabashedly patriotic. She flies the flag on her front porch all year. She celebrates the Fourth of July for several days. She wears tee shirts with images of flags, fireworks, "I (heart) America," and "Born in the USA." She makes cupcakes topped with red, white, and blue sprinkles. She serves up hot dogs and hamburgers, and the *pièce de résistance*—for the family picnic at Rawley Park, a cake frosted like the flag. All-American food for my all-American grandmother.

Gram's grandparents settled in a tiny Minnesota town of immigrants. "Remember this?" Gram asked, holding an old photo of her grandfather and his neighbors in their little town, posing with the American flag on a long-ago Fourth of July.

"I remember, Gram," I said.

"Salt of the earth they were," Gram said with a smile. "Did you know my grandfather was a gymnast in the old country?"

I nodded. Gram needs to tell her stories, and she needs me to listen.

"He did tricks in the backyard on the clothesline pole. Do you even know what that is?"

I laughed. "Yes, Gram, I've seen pictures of clotheslines."

In Three Rivers, it seems the whole town gathers at Rawley Park on Forchuly. Baseball games—Kiwanians versus the Rotarians, Lions versus Elks. A little train runs on a track for the kiddies. A museum at the park celebrates the pioneer history of Three Rivers, with demonstrations of weaving, butter churning, and a log-splitting contest.

And at the end of the day, the community band plays a concert of patriotic songs in the Bowl—our version of the Hollywood Bowl. After dark, there is, of course, a fireworks display.

Families come early in the day to stake out a picnic spot. The smell of burgers and hot dogs on the grill. Laughter and squeals from the playground. Kids with sparklers. A family playing volleyball over a net strung between two trees. A dog chasing a frisbee. Fathers and sons playing catch. Grandparents in lawn chairs, looking on smiling. Infants in strollers, napping in the shade.

This year, our family would be at the park by noon. Gram and Nathan. Greg, Sarah, and their three children. My sister Deanne with her husband and their four. My mother. And now, likely Duncan.

"I'd love to hear more," I said, "but I have to get to work." I hugged them both, took Moe, and headed out.

Moe and I opened the office at ten. Five minutes later, the little girl, Louisa, came in carrying a birdcage with a blue parakeet in it.

She grinned. "He came back! Banjo came back! All by himself!"

I clapped my hands. "Yay for Banjo! He found his way home, and all by himself, huh? What a smart bird!" I looked at Louisa's mother, who stood behind her daughter. She shrugged and gave me a look.

I knew that look. *Rover's gone to live at a lovely farm in the country. Yes, Virginia, there is a Santa Claus.* The lies we tell children.

Louisa frowned. "He's smart but, he forgot how to talk."

I said, "Sometimes people forget things, and pets do too. I once had a dog who forgot to go outside to go potty." I wrinkled my nose. "I had to teach him again."

She giggled. "I'll just teach Banjo again."

Her mother said, "She insisted on coming to show you that Banjo came back. She didn't want you to keep looking."

"I appreciate that." I looked at Louisa. "So, as the detective, I'm going to say, 'Case closed.' Is that okay with you, Louisa?"

Louisa agreed, and her mother escorted her out the door. As I made myself a coffee, I thought about what mothers do for their children. Anything to keep them safe and happy. Well, good mothers do that.

My cup of coffee had just finished brewing when the back door opened, and Larry came in with Chief Bronson on the other end of the leash.

"Down," the chief said, and Larry flopped down in the middle of the tile floor. "Good boy," the chief said. "I'm teaching him some commands."

"He's got that one nailed," I said. Laying down is one of old Larry's best tricks.

Moe came to sniff everybody. Satisfied we were all still friends, Moe plopped on the floor next to Larry.

The chief smiled at me. "G'mornin', Chickie. That coffee smells good. When you're done, I'll make myself one."

The chief understands the office protocol. He doesn't treat me like a servant. He makes his own coffee. I appreciate that.

I asked him about the money Lou found in the urn.

With a shrug, he said, "Hers to keep, fair and square. She bought the unit and all its contents. The money's hers, no question."

A happy ending—for Lou, anyway. Not so happy for Bernard Weatherby, who let the cash-filled urn go. As Lou would say, his trash became her treasure.

I called her to tell her the good news. I figured she'd be at the store, just opening up. She didn't answer.

Since it was such a lovely morning, I decided to walk the few blocks down River Street to her store to tell her in person.

CHAPTER FORTY

THE FRONT DOOR TO Lou's Vintage was still locked. Past time for her to open. I put my hands against the front window and peered inside. The lights were off, but I could see that the store was a mess.

Carnage. Glass cases smashed, jewelry and dishes tossed around. Bookshelves toppled over. Clothing stripped off hangers, thrown into piles.

Just then, two figures stumbled out from the back room to the front of the store. A man, burly, tall. His hands around a woman's neck, shaking her.

I pounded on the glass. "Lou!"

The man looked at me and shook Lou harder.

I ran around to the back of the building. The back door stood open. I heard the man yell as I ran inside.

"Where's the damn urn? Give it to me?"

Lou pounded her fists against his chest, fighting for air.

I yelled from behind him. "She can't tell you if she's dead!"

He threw Lou to the floor. She crawled away from him, coughing, trying to breathe. He turned to face me.

I said, "You must be Bernard Weatherby." Who else would care about the urn?

He growled, "Who the hell are you?"

"Mackenzie Prentice."

Recognition dawned. "You're the snoop. The manager told me you were trying to track me down." He pointed at Lou. "Told me she bought my stuff. I need that urn!"

Remain calm. Keep him talking. "What's so important about a bunch of ashes? Who is it?"

"My uncle. He meant a lot to me."

What a liar. "Why didn't you just ask Lou for the urn?"

Bernard Weatherby didn't notice Lou had gotten to her feet and was creeping up behind him, holding a vintage crockpot high.

He turned just as she swung at him, grabbed the crockpot, and wrenched it from her. He swung it into her solar plexus. Lou doubled over, clutching her stomach, groaning.

He came at me, swinging the crockpot toward my head.

I dodged. He gave a howl of anger and lunged at me again.

I ducked behind a glass display case that hadn't been smashed yet.

He brought the crockpot down against the top, and the glass shattered into a million bits. I shielded my eyes from the spraying shards as I ran out from behind the case, glass crunching under my feet.

I looked around for anything to use as a weapon or a shield. Lou's precious Dior dress was in a heap on the floor. The mannequin that had been wearing it stood naked.

I wrapped my arms around the mannequin. "Let's go, girl!" I said and ran, full speed, toward Bernard.

The dummy's head flew off as I rammed into him. He lost his balance. Dropped the crockpot as he went down hard. Bernard hit his head on the corner of a table as he fell. He lay still, bleeding from his temple.

I heard sirens. I went over to Lou. "You okay?"

She nodded and sat back against the wall and gestured to the alarm button on the underside of the counter.

"You pushed it?"

She nodded and gave a little smile.

I took Lou's keys and unlocked the front door. A minute later, Officer Burns arrived with several of Three Rivers's finest and a couple EMTs.

Burns and I go way back—to last fall. He looked at me. "You again?" he said. Burns is okay, if you don't mind obnoxious.

I gave a little salute. "Nice to see you too, Officer Burns." I explained the situation to him. Bernard Weatherby had come around as an EMT bandaged his forehead. Burns gave the order to cuff him and cart him away. While the EMTs checked Lou and me over, Officer Burns took notes.

Lou told him she'd found the store trashed when she arrived that morning. Bernard had broken in earlier, and when he couldn't find the urn, he went berserk.

Lou caught him in the act. "He threatened me! I'd have given it to him if he'd asked politely," she said. "But I refused, and he got violent. That's when Mackenzie arrived." She looked at me and squeezed my hand. "Thank God!"

Burns closed his notebook after we promised to sign formal statements later.

Everyone gone, Lou sat in a 1950s imitation Eames chair, leaned forward, and put her head in her hands.

I asked, "So if Bernard knew the money was there, why did he leave the urn in the storage unit?"

She looked up. "He told me that his father was a gambler, and his mother hated that. His father won big, hid the money, and told Bernard that he could have it if he could find it. Bernard called it . . ." She paused, thinking. "He called it 'that sick bastard's version of a treasure hunt.'" She nodded. "Yes, that's what he called it. Anyway, he must have searched through everything in the house after his mother died. He said that urn with his uncle's ashes was right there on the fireplace mantel. He never thought to look there."

She stood and looked around. "Oh, God. Look at this place. What a mess."

I surveyed the damage. Bric-a-brac, thingamabobs, and whatchamacallits strewn across the floor. "Where do we even start?"

Lou stood, picked up the mannequin's head from where it had rolled, and reunited it with the body. She crunched through broken glass as she carried the dummy across the store and stood it in its former place.

She looked down and gave a little strangled sound. She stooped by the dress on the floor and sniffed it. "Oh my God! He *peed* on this!" She picked it up by the edge of the fabric and turned to me, enraged. "What kind of animal does this?" She shook the dress, and little drops of urine flew. "Who pees on a Dior? It's a *Dee-YORE,* for God's sake!"

Who indeed?

Lou rejected my idea that we lock up and go find some breakfast. "I need to get this cleaned up," she said.

I got on my cell and texted for reinforcements.

Lou and I got started, and within thirty minutes, help arrived. Gram came with her friends Velma and Estelle, who'd been enjoying their usual Monday morning coffee at Hilda's Café. My pal Tansy canceled a yoga class to come and help, bringing five of the class members with her.

I'd texted my mother's friend Doris from the Oven Fresh Bakery. Doris had called Lauren and her husband, Mike, owners of Java Java. They'd texted Chelsea and Glory from Of All Things, the shop next to TriMak.

The Three Rivers Small Business Association rallied, thanks to the grapevine, and came to the aid of one of their own. This is how it is in Three Rivers. People care.

CHAPTER FORTY-ONE

L OU'S SHOP WAS COMING together, thanks to all the help. Walking back to TriMak, I thought about Bernard Weatherby looking for "treasure." I was on a treasure hunt myself, looking for Maisie Gordon's necklace—a treasure to her dying mother.

A shiny black Lincoln Town Car was parked in front of TriMak. Trip, Sheena, and Chief Bronson were in the front reception area talking with an old man in a wheelchair. Germany was sitting at my desk. Moe, Larry, and Curly were curled up together in the corner.

The old man—probably in his eighties—had a fringe of white hair and a sour look. He wore a three-piece suit, which had to be miserable in this heat. His eyes were sharp behind thick lenses. A liveried chauffeur stood behind the chair.

The chief said, "Ah, Mackenzie. This is Wallace McCrae."

"Nice to meet you, sir," I said. He ignored my proffered hand.

He frowned at the chief and barked, "I want to know what progress has been made in finding out for certain what happened to my granddaughter."

I didn't need to be a genius to put two and two together. Mrs. Gordon's father. The grandfather who hired Sheena.

Sheena jumped in. "I've made good progress, sir. Following up on lots of leads. Should have an answer any day now."

She's completely bluffing. Snarky relished seeing Sheena on the hot seat.

The old man glared at her. "Well, my daughter doesn't have time for 'any day.' I need answers." He shot a disdainful look at the dogs, then addressed the chief. "What kind of outfit are you running here?"

Before the chief could answer, the old man spoke over his shoulder to his chauffeur. "Ferguson, I ran a tight unit, didn't I? No nonsense in our unit, isn't that right, Ferguson?"

The chauffeur gave a quick bow of his head and clicked his heels. "Yes, General McCrae. You ran a very tight unit. No nonsense. Yes, sir."

Ah. This former military man—a general, no less—was obviously used to having people jump when he ordered them to do so. I wondered how his family felt about that.

Trip spoke. "I'm sure Sheena will be able to provide what you need." He looked at her, pleading in his eyes. "By the end of business today? Right, Sheena?"

She stammered, her face reddening. "Well, it might take a little longer than that."

I piped up. "Sir, uh, General, sir—" I wasn't sure what the protocol should be. The old man shifted in his chair and fixed his eyes on me. A trickle of sweat ran down my back.

I swallowed hard and plunged forward. "I've been interviewing her friends, and I've done a very thorough search of the area where Maisie died. I'm interviewing her teachers and her classmates. I have a very strong lead, and I may be able to give you a definitive answer soon. Maybe by the end of today or at least in the next couple of days. I know Mrs. Gordon, uh, your daughter, needs an answer. I'll be working around the clock for your family, sir." I almost saluted.

He looked at me for a long moment. "So *you're* the one working this case?"

The chief spoke, his voice firm and authoritative. "It's an *agency* matter. We're a *team* here." He glanced at me and smiled. "And Mackenzie here is one of our strongest operatives. I have complete confidence—"

Sheena's hand shot up, interrupting the chief. "General McCrae, *I'm* the one with experience here. You hired *me* to do this job, and I'm confident that *I'll* have answers for you."

The old man waited a long moment, looking at each of us in turn. Finally, he spoke. "I don't care who gets the answers as long as we get them quickly. Keep me informed." He gestured to Ferguson, who snapped to attention and wheeled him out to the Lincoln.

I looked at the chief and started to thank him for his confidence. Before I could say it, he got in Sheena's face. "Ms. Shay! That was completely uncalled for. What you said to him was out of line!"

Sheena stared at Chief Bronson, a line of sweat forming on her upper lip. Her eyes flashed, her jaw set. *Is she actually going to take him on?* I was pretty sure disrespecting authority contributed to her getting fired in The City. I had a moment of hope that maybe she'd blow it and the chief would send her packing.

Good riddance to bad rubbish, Snarky said.

I noticed Trip squeezing Sheena's arm, no doubt offering a warning to bite her tongue. She got it. "Sorry, sir. I'm grateful to be able to work with you." She looked at me. "*All* of you."

If she'd said that without sneering, I might have believed her.

The chief said, "That's better. Let's all work together here and get this job done for this family. Okay? Trip? Sheena? Chickie? Germany? Okay?"

We all nodded. The chief is kind of like Gram—when he tells you to do something, you do it.

CHAPTER FORTY-TWO

TOOK FOUR OF THE remaining list of twenty boys with B names and divided the rest among Trip, Sheena, Chief Bronson, and Germany. Four names each.

Trip asked, "Why are we doing this?"

I explained. "Whoever this person is, they might have insight into Maisie's state of mind. Maybe she confessed her feelings, and he rejected her. Maybe that caused her to—" I stopped. Germany had paled. Thinking about his sister, I assumed. "Uh, caused her to be depressed. We just want to cover all the bases."

Trip nodded understanding.

The chief said, "Okay, let's get this thing resolved. Time's a-wasting."

With coffees all around, we got busy tracking people. At the end of an hour, we'd come up empty. The ones we'd been able to reach remembered Maisie—the death of a classmate tends to stick with you. Nobody admitted to a romantic involvement with her. Of course, she might not have told the mystery boy about her crush. And of course, any one of them could be lying.

Next, I gave out the names of Maisie's teachers I'd found on her report cards. Another hour passed. The others had come up empty. Teachers who remembered her didn't know about her mystery boy.

I had one name left—Miss Harada, my English teacher and Maisie's homeroom teacher. She still lived in Three Rivers and answered on the third ring. She said she remembered me, and I explained what I needed.

"Of course, I remember Maisie. That poor child. So tragic. She used to come to my classroom after school and talk to me. I felt so sorry for her. She lost her father so early, you know? But she wasn't depressed, and I never understood why she would take her own life."

My Spidey senses tingled, and I asked Miss Harada if she had time to talk in person. She did. I headed to her house at the bottom of the West Hill.

"You've grown up, Mackenzie."

"And you look exactly the same, Miss Harada."

"Please call me Ema." Like the American name Emma.

"I can't do that," I said with a smile. "You'll always be Miss Harada to me."

She nodded understanding. Miss Harada looked just as she had twenty years before. Five feet tall, tops. Same straight, black hair framing her round face. Small hands clasping mine in greeting. Her simple gray dress hung loosely over her slim frame above fabric-strapped thong sandals with thick cork soles.

Her Japanese roots were evident in her decor. Paper scrolls decorated her living room walls. The low table in front of the couch held a red vase with a single dark red flower, a long green frond and another branch with pods hanging from it.

I pointed at it. "That's so interesting." *Make small talk. Put the person at ease.*

She smiled. "Yes. Ikebana. Japanese flower arranging. It's a hobby of mine."

I pointed to Japanese letters on a painted scroll. "And what is that?"

"An ancient poem. A tale of love and heartbreak," she said.

"It's beautiful."

She nodded. "Beautiful, yes, but a tragic tale. Fascinating, isn't it, what artists can come up with? Art, poetry, fiction. The stories that people invent. So interesting."

I'd heard lots of stories from victims and from suspects since I'd started investigating. Hard to tell fact from fiction at times. And sometimes I didn't know the truth until all was said and done. But there was a special thrill when the pieces fell together. An addicting thrill.

Miss Harada asked, "Would you care for tea? Hot or iced?"

"No, thanks. I don't have much time. Can we talk about Maisie Gordon?"

She smiled. "Maisie loved to write. Stories of romance and suspense. She was quite gifted, as I recall."

I explained the urgency with Mrs. Gordon's health.

Miss Harada hesitated. "The things Maisie told me in confidence—" She closed her eyes for a moment, then looked at me. "I suppose that doesn't matter anymore, does it?"

"Her mother needs to know."

"Sit, please. I will tell you what I remember."

We sat side by side on her small couch. Miss Harada spoke softly. "Maisie was in love with someone she said was unattainable. An older boy."

"Did she tell you who it was?"

"No, she didn't. She just referred to him by the initial B."

"Did you ever see them together at school?"

She shook her head. "No, I never did. And now that I think about it, somehow, I got the impression he wasn't at our school. Maybe he was at another school, or maybe he'd already graduated."

Rational Me didn't like the sound of that. Not. At. All. *Another school? Already graduated? Where would I even start?*

"Is there anything else?"

She frowned, thinking. "Yes, she slipped once and almost said his name. She caught herself and said that B was for his nickname."

That was all Miss Harada remembered.

I thanked her and left. Trip's BMW was at the curb outside, with Sheena at the wheel, scrolling on her phone. I walked to the BMW and rapped on the passenger's side window. Sheena jumped, then lowered the window.

I leaned inside. "You have nothing better to do than follow me around town?"

She huffed. "I have leads of my own. Besides, it's a free country." She started the car. "Step back, or I'll take your head off."

I had barely gotten out of the way before she floored it.

So much for cooperation.

Driving back to the office, I reviewed the case. If the B stood for a nickname, we'd wasted a ton of time tracking boys with B first names for nothing. I certainly didn't want to explain this to "the team." And what if the boy wasn't from Three Rivers High or had already graduated? Too many possibilities. Overwhelming.

I smacked my palm against the steering wheel. "What the heck am I supposed to do now?"

Jimbo chirped. He had no idea what I should do next either.

CHAPTER FORTY-THREE

JUST BEFORE QUITTING TIME on Monday, Ralph Quentin called our office. He'd fractured his hip badly when he fell. He'd had surgery and would be at the hospital for a few days, then at Drury's Rest for a month of rehab.

He asked, "Can you please take care of the boys? Take in my mail? And maybe clean out my fridge? Help yourself to whatever's in there."

I assured him we'd take care of everything, wished him a speedy recovery, and hung up. I texted the update to Trip and the chief, then ordered flowers for Ralph from all of us.

I looked down at Moe—at my feet as usual—and told him the good news. "You're mine for the duration. Okay with you?"

His whole body wagged, and I swear he smiled. Moe and I locked up and headed home.

Duncan was at Gram's dinner table that night. He and my mother seemed better than ever. My mother fed him a forkful of chicken. He shared one of his green beans with her. She giggled.

Snarky thought it was a bit much. *I swear if they start grooming each other, I'll puke.*

At dessert time, Duncan had his arm around her at the table, and she leaned into him as they shared a bowl of maple nut ice cream. One bowl, two spoons.

Lonely Me looked on, a little envious. Even Snarky was quiet.

After dinner, my mother left with Duncan. We all knew that meant she'd be at his place for the night. I offered to take cleanup duty so Gram and Nathan could relax.

The dishes done, I snapped off the kitchen light, and Moe and I headed out to the carriage house.

I set my laptop on my new dining table and logged onto an online site for high school yearbooks. I pulled up the Three Rivers yearbook for the year my older sister Stephanie graduated, which was a year ahead of Charity Gordon. If Maisie did indeed have a crush on an older boy, maybe he was in Steph's class.

Snarky snarked. *Duh! Genius. Why didn't you think of this before?*

I started to set up a fake account using Stephanie's name and birth date.

Rational Me said flatly, *This is wrong. Like identity theft.*

Anxious Me had more to say. *Wrong! Wrong! Wrong! Your sister will be soooo maaaaaad if she finds out.* She still fears my big sister's wrath.

Rational Me suggested I call Steph and ask for permission to go snooping in her name. *Or she might have ideas about who the boy could be, and you won't have to snoop at all.*

I called, and we chatted a bit. No, Steph wasn't coming home on Thursday for the family picnic. She'd be spending the Fourth of July with Mason, the wealthy man twenty years her senior she dated. Do you call him her "boyfriend"? Or maybe "partner"? I wasn't sure.

"We're taking his boat down the river for the long weekend," she said. His "boat" is actually a yacht, and the river they'd be cruising down would be the Mississippi.

After small talk, I asked, "Do you recall any boys in your class, or maybe a year ahead of you or behind, with nicknames starting with B?"

"Okay, first of all—weird question."

I explained about Maisie.

Stephanie thought a moment, then said, "Well, there was a boy we called 'Boogie.' Can't remember why. Also, a year ahead of me was a guy we called Buzz. He sat behind me in trigonometry. Super smart. His last name was Aldrin, so what else would we call him? You know. Buzz Aldrin."

"Yeah. The astronaut."

"Uh-huh. And, of course, there was Boomer."

"Who?"

"Boomer. Zach Carson. He was in my class."

My heart raced. I thanked Stephanie and hung up.

It was almost eleven. Too late to call Greta Bullfinch. I'd have to wait until morning. I shut off the lights and headed upstairs to the bedroom loft.

Sometime later, a crash of thunder woke me from a dream about Nick Milcross. Lovely dream. Rude awakening.

I checked the time on my phone—2:35 a.m. Another peal of thunder, close enough to shake the loft. Moe gave a whimper and jumped up onto the bed. Chloe hissed at him and jumped onto the pillow next to mine.

Lightning illuminated the loft bedroom. I'd fallen asleep with the big window open to allow the cooler night air inside.

Rain pelted me through the screen as I closed the window, muffling the noise of the storm.

I was wide awake. I turned the switch on the bedside lamp. Nothing. The power was out. I used my phone's flashlight to light my way down the stairs, Moe following behind.

I flicked the kitchen light switch. Nothing. Why do we do that? We know the power is out, but we check again. And again.

I was thirsty. I opened the refrigerator. No light. *Duh.* Just as I grabbed a bottle of water, lightning illuminated the kitchen, followed immediately by a bang of thunder and a loud cracking sound coming from upstairs. I dropped the water as the whole house shook. Moe dove under the couch.

Heart pounding, I went up the steps. The higher I got, the louder the storm sounded. Cold wind blew down from above. My head just above the top of the stairs, I looked up as a burst of lightning lit my bedroom. A huge hunk of maple tree had fallen through the roof, taking out the far corner of the room. Rain poured in.

"Chloe! Where are you? Come here, kitty, kitty!"

I didn't dare go farther into the room. Another part of the tree might fall. I didn't know if the floor was safe to walk on. The entire loft might be compromised. There was going to be significant water damage. Anxious Me could freak out later. Right now, finding Chloe was the priority.

"Chloe!" I called her again and heard a meow from under the bed. I shined the phone flashlight toward her and patted my hand on the floor. "Come here, kitty. It's okay."

Another meow and Chloe ran past me and down the steps. I followed her. I grabbed my hoodie from a hook by the entry door, draped it over my head, and Chloe, Moe, and I hightailed it together to Gram's.

Gram's kitchen door was unlocked, as usual. I flicked the kitchen light switch. Power was out here as well. The whole neighborhood was probably in the dark.

I got a flashlight from a kitchen drawer, saving my phone battery, and headed upstairs.

The door was closed to Gram and Nathan's bedroom. I peeked in. They were sleeping soundly. My mother was at Duncan's.

Chloe and Moe followed me into the Rose Room, where I climbed into the cozy comfort of the big bed. The room was warm, but I was chilled from running in the rain. I pulled the covers to my chin. Chloe curled up next to me as Moe settled on the bed at my feet.

I listened as the storm sounds became more distant. The rain would stop soon, I hoped, and maybe the damage to the carriage house wasn't as bad as I feared.

Whatever the damage was, Nick would be able to fix it. I was sure of that. And that meant we'd spend more time together. And everything would be just fine.

"Everything will be just fine," I whispered into the darkness. I put that thought on repeat, not believing it no matter how many times I said it.

CHAPTER FORTY-FOUR

Tuesday, July 2

THE SUN, BRIGHT AGAINST the window shade, woke me around eight. The Rose Room felt stifling and humid already. I'd kicked the covers off sometime in the night. Chloe and Moe were gone, probably seeking cooler places to be.

I tested the bedside lamp. Still no power.

I got up and went to the bathroom. My toothbrush was in the carriage house, so I put toothpaste on my index finger and rubbed my teeth. Rinsed and spit, then splashed cold water on my face. I checked my reflection. I looked a fright. I combed through my hair with my damp fingers. No improvement.

I took my cell and padded downstairs in my jammies to the kitchen.

Gram was at the counter in her nightgown and fuzzy slippers, with the smiley faces across the toes—a gift from one of the great-grandkids last Christmas. She was opening a can of salmon in the light from the window above the kitchen sink.

Moe sat at her feet. His love and loyalty are freely given to anyone with food.

"Morning, Gram," I said, hugging her from behind.

She rolled her shoulders and pushed me back with her elbow. "Too hot for hugs." Not like Gram at all. The heat was making us all cranky.

She put the salmon into a bowl, and before she set it on the table, she tossed a little piece to Moe. She frowned at me. "What are you doing here? I thought you were in the carriage house."

I told her about the tree crashing into my bedroom.

"Oh, dear Lord!" She hugged me, a sticky but comforting-like-Gram hug. "Are you okay?"

I assured her that Chloe, Moe, and I were fine, but Nick was going to have to repair the damage. "Okay if I bunk here for the duration?"

"Of course. You're always welcome." She brought a box of saltines, a jar of Jif extra crunchy, paper plates, and silverware to the table. "Power's out, so no coffee. Too hot for coffee anyway." She wiped the back of her hand across her forehead. "I don't even want to open the refrigerator. Need to save whatever cold is still in there."

I made myself a stack of peanut butter and cracker sandwiches and handed one to Moe.

My mother came into the kitchen, swearing under her breath.

"I thought you were at Duncan's, Mom."

"He brought me home after the storm passed. I have a second interview at Citizen's Bank this morning, and my hair is a mess. But I can't wash it because I can't dry it. Of all days! Damn it!"

Cranky.

Gram cleared her throat. "Watch your language." Her roof, her rules, no matter how old you are.

My mother grumbled what sounded like, "Sorry, Mother."

Behind Gram's back, I shook my finger at my mother and mouthed, "Naughty, naughty."

She stuck her tongue out at me. *Real mature, Mom.*

My mom grabbed a couple of crackers and said, "I'm going to ask Duncan to come and get me. Assuming his power is on." She headed back upstairs.

Gram smiled. "So glad they worked things out."

I looked at my phone. Battery was thirty percent. No way I'd be able to charge it at home. I opened the local weather app. "Stuart Klump says ninety-five today and thunderstorms again. National Weather Service has another extreme heat warning."

"Good gravy!" Gram said. "This weather is relentless." She sat and piled salmon on a cracker.

"It's scorching," I said.

"Blistering," Gram said.

We continued trading synonyms. It's what we do.

"Sweltering," I said.

She countered with, "It's boiling."

I offered, "Stifling."

"It's hotter than the middle kettle of hell," Gram said with finality.

"Ooh, watch *your* language," I teased.

"That's what your grandfather used to say." She smiled at the memory of Papa Powell. "I still miss him."

"I do too," I said. I stood and gave her a light hug. I finished the last of my peanut butter and cracker sandwiches. "I'm going to the carriage house to check the damage."

She looked at my bare feet. "Take my slippers," she said and slid them off.

My toes were warm inside the fleece-lined slippers, resting in the indentations of Gram's toes. I don't know why, but Gram giving me her slippers choked me up. I hugged her again—a little longer this time—and went out the back door.

Leaves, sticks, and small branches littered the parking pad behind the house and the sidewalk and lawn between the Victorian and the carriage house. One large branch on the maple in the middle of the yard had broken halfway. It dangled precariously over the swing set that had been there forever, now serving the next generation of Gram's family.

The carriage house door was ajar. I evidently hadn't pulled it closed when Chloe, Moe, and I made our escape. I stepped inside into a weird silence—no refrigerator running. You don't notice the sounds of a household until they're not there.

I heard water dripping, coming from the bathroom in the far corner. I checked. Half the bathroom ceiling had darkened. Water dripped from several spots along the drywall seams and the edges of the light/fan fixture. I imagined the ceiling saturated with water and crashing to the floor, bringing the bathroom above with it.

I went up the stairs just far enough to take a look at the loft. Morning light filled my bedroom. Shingles littered the floor in the far corner in front of my closet, where a huge chunk of maple tree rested on the floor.

Water covered half the bedroom floor. I'd hoped to grab some clothes from the closet, but they were probably soaked, and I wasn't about to risk walking across the bedroom.

My luxury vinyl plank flooring was probably ruined. It had been chosen so carefully on a shopping trip with Nick, where we, like an old married couple, had searched together for the perfect shade of gray—the perfect flooring for my perfect little nest.

Damn it! Badass was not happy.

Be grateful you're alive, Rational offered.

Anxious felt a knot in her stomach. *Ohmigod we could have been crushed to death.* I started to shake. I tapped Nick's number on my cell. He picked up right away.

My voice close to breaking, I filled him in.

He got serious. "You okay?"

I said I was, even though I wasn't. "I'm staying at Gram's."

"I'll be right there," he said. "Sit tight."

I pulled the carriage house door shut and picked my way back through the debris to the Victorian.

I borrowed a sports bra, socks, and undies from my mother, along with a decent-looking shirt and a nice pair of shorts. She gave me a pair of running socks and her old ISO Triumph running shoes. "You can keep the shoes if you want. I just got a new pair." She puts in a lot of running miles and replaces her running shoes every year. The shoes pinched my feet a little bit, but beggars can't be choosers.

While I waited for Nick, I gave my parakeets, Tweet and Chirp, fresh seed and water. They don't seem to mind the heat. They're happy living by the big window in Gram's front parlor, chirping and tweeting all day as they watch the wild birds outside. I hadn't decided yet if I wanted to move them to the carriage house. And certainly not now. They'd had trauma enough surviving the apartment fire. They didn't need any tree branches falling on them.

Rational Me whispered, *Illogical. Catastrophizing.*

Anxious Me countered, *You never know.*

Tansy talks about that "never knowing" thing all the time. The fact is we never know what will happen next in life. "We must learn to be okay with uncertainty," she tells me.

Easy for Tansy to say. She grew up on the West Hill. Top of the hill. Upper-upper-crusty. How much uncertainty has she faced? She's had enough money, support, and opportunities her whole life. And she has a killer body, great hair, and is gorgeous. Lucky her.

I grew up without that kind of certainty. My mom did her best, but there were times when we didn't have the money or the means to get the things we needed. Gram came to the rescue a lot, but it's not the same. My mother was always anxious, and she passed that on to me. So, being "okay with uncertainty" doesn't come naturally.

Alone in Gram's kitchen, I stood at the sink, looking out the window at the carriage house. It looked okay from this angle, but what was going to happen?

Anxious Me started whipping up worst-case scenarios. *The whole thing might have to be demolished. We'll never have our own place. Never have a love life again. We'll die alone and our seventeen cats will eat us.*

Ridiculous, I know. But that's how it goes.

I heard Tansy in my head. "Breathe in for a count of four, hold for five, then breathe out for six." I closed my eyes and inhaled, held it, then let it out slowly. A couple more rounds of breath and I felt a little better.

Rational Me knows that things work out eventually.

I heard a rap at the back door and turned to see Nick's face smiling at me through the glass. Relief flooded my body. I opened the door and grabbed him.

He held me tight. Or I held him. Hard to be sure.

CHAPTER FORTY-FIVE

NICK MURMURED REASSURANCE. "IT'S going to be okay. It'll be okay." After a few minutes, I felt better and let him go.

"Thanks for coming," I said. *We feel better when Nick is around,* Lonely whispered.

Nick smiled. "We had damage at a couple other projects last night, too, but I'll check your place and call you later." He headed for the carriage house.

I needed to get to the office. As I drove toward River Street, I was relieved to see that house lights were on, and River Street businesses were open. Power would no doubt be back on at Gram's soon.

Jimbo chirped as I drove, and to take my mind off the disaster at home, I focused on the case. Maisie was dead. Her mother was dying. Her sister wasn't any help. Maybe Miss Harada was mistaken about the boy being older. The mysterious B could be William "Buddy" Carson. He was Maisie's age. Maybe Maisie thought it would be fun if she and her sister both married Carson boys. Maybe she imagined a double wedding—romance novel style. Or, if the boy was older, he might be Buzz, or Boogie, or Jemma's boyfriend, Bubba.

I drove toward the office, dodging a couple of downed tree limbs and two garbage cans the storm had rolled into the street.

I asked Jimbo, "What do you think of that grandfather—the general? Yikes. Scary dude, right? And what's Ferguson's story?"

Jimbo had no opinion.

I thought about Miss Harada's suggestion that the boy might have gone to a different school. That opened up so many more possibilities—a mind-boggling number of options. Impossible. Greta Bullfinch wouldn't talk, and besides, whatever her "secret" was, it probably had nothing at all to do with Maisie.

I pounded the steering wheel. "Dead ends. Dead ends. Nothing but dead ends!"

Jimbo gave a chirp of sympathy. Nice to have a cricket who is so understanding.

My cell buzzed. A text from Tansy asking me to stop by her studio. Nobody was in the studio area when I got there. I called out. "Tansy? It's Mack."

Tansy poked her head out of the small kitchenette in the back of the studio. "Come on back here. We're just having tea."

I walked to Tansy's back room. Her little white table with three chairs was set with three cups, a tea bag steeping in each. I felt like Goldilocks.

Tansy was there with a tall, thin woman with a strong, yoga body like Tansy's. Bleached white hair cut short. Purple streak through the left side. Mid-forties maybe.

I took the empty seat.

"Mack, this is my friend Topaz. She's a yoga teacher too. We met at a training a couple years ago."

"Cool name," I said.

"My real name is Lucille, after my grandma. Topaz was my stage name."

She just got a lot more interesting. "Stage? You're an actress?"

She and Tansy exchanged a look, and Topaz laughed. "Nope. This stage had a pole."

Really interesting. "I've, uh, never met an exotic dancer before."

Topaz laughed. "Let's just call it what it is. I was a stripper."

"Okay, I've never met a stripper before."

She laid her hand on my arm. "Well, honey, you have now."

The three of us laughed.

I asked, "How did you come up with Topaz for a stage name?"

She took a sip of tea and settled back to tell the tale. "Well, after high school, I was drifting around, and I met this guy. He was older. His name was Armand, but everybody called him Ziggy. Anyway, Ziggy looks into my eyes one day." She leaned forward so I could see her eyes. "Look at my eyes. You see? They're brown, but they have little glints of yellow light. See that?"

I looked. I saw. "Yep."

"Anyway, he says my eyes remind him of the way a topaz sparkles in the sun." She got wistful. "He said my eyes were beautiful. Like topaz. I told him that was amazing because my birthday is in November, and topaz is my birthstone."

Her voice dropped to a whisper as a dark cloud passed over her face. "Nobody ever told me anything about me was beautiful until he said that."

Topaz fell silent, sipping her tea, probably wrestling whatever demons that memory had brought up.

Tansy said, "Mack, when I talked to my mother, she said something about a scandal back in the day. I don't know if it's connected to Maisie Gordon. Something about the place Topaz worked. Tell her, Topaz."

Topaz said, "I used to dance at this place south of town— Man Alive, it was called. Out on the highway, between here and Campbell. I danced there before I got clean—fifteen years ago now. I got into meditation and yoga for sobriety."

I'd heard tales about the place. I knew the chief was involved in shutting it down.

She continued. "I was there that night when the cops raided the place. Lots of serious sh—sorry, stuff going down."

"Did you get arrested?"

"No. Me and the other girls just gave our statements. They had enough on the owner to shut the whole place down without us having to testify."

"Scary," I said.

"You bet your fanny. Never saw so much firepower in one place. Like SWAT coming down on you. Funny thing was, about ten minutes before the cops busted in, a bunch of the regulars left the place."

Tansy said, "That's what my mom remembered hearing."

I said, "Someone tipped them off."

Topaz said, "Yup. They scattered like roaches at the first whiff of Raid." She laughed. "Raid? Roaches? Get it?"

I smiled. "I get it. Who were those regulars?"

Topaz frowned. "You'd be amazed if I told you. Guys who would not be happy if they knew that I knew what they did back then."

My investigator senses tingled. "Things like what, exactly?"

"Drugs, sex with minors. Stuff. Reputations could be ruined."

Tansy broke in. "My mother said there were rumors, but she didn't know who—"

Topaz interrupted her. "High muckety-mucks who wouldn't be too happy if certain things were made known. You get my drift?"

"Muckety-mucks? In Three Rivers? Like who?"

Topaz leaned toward me. "Let me just say some of those people up there on the Hill aren't who you think they are."

I looked at Tansy. She nodded.

I turned back to Topaz. "And if you were going to name names?"

She held up a hand. "I can't say who was there for sure, not after all this time. And besides, I'm no snitch. I like my head right where it is, thank you very much."

"So you think they'd hurt you if you told?"

"No question about it. Probably. Maybe."

I wondered who in Three Rivers would be willing to hurt someone or even kill someone to keep a secret. I'd had encounters with killers—for greed, for revenge, for their own sick reasons. Who would kill to protect a reputation? For the sake of their ego?

I told her about Maisie Gordon, how her mother needed answers.

"I remember hearing about that. Must be tough for her mother." She went on talking about the other dancers—girls like her who were addicts, others who were runaways. "Everybody had a story, you know. Lots of abuse and trauma back there for all of us. Some turn to drugs. Some decide it's not worth living anymore."

I didn't press. Talking about your trauma doesn't make it any better. Whatever Topaz was doing to cope these days was working, and I didn't need to dredge up the past.

Tansy said, "So, I just thought you'd want to hear about the raid from Topaz. My mom thought it might have something to do with the Gordons, but she wasn't sure."

I said, "I'm having trouble connecting the dots here, Tans."

"You'll figure it out. You're so good at that stuff." Tansy had more confidence in my abilities than I had at that moment. But that's what friends are for.

I thanked Topaz for her time and Tansy for the tea and took off for TriMak.

The chief was in his office, tying more flies, when I got there. I told him what I'd heard at Tansy's.

He leaned back in his chair and crossed his arms. "I remember that night very well. Coordinated effort with Clearwater County Sheriff's Department and the state DOJ. Big deal."

"Wasn't it weird that the regulars got out before the cops got there?"

He got quiet. "Yeah, we couldn't figure out who tipped them off."

"But somebody did?"

"Most definitely."

"Who knew about the raid?"

"Just the team, but that's a lot of moving parts. Could have been anyone on the team."

"Who authorized the raid?"

"Judge Carson signed off on the order."

My wheels turned in an uncomfortable direction. "What if—"

Chief Bronson held up a hand. "Stop right there, Mackenzie. I told you before that Rollo Carson's integrity is beyond scrutiny. Do not—I repeat, do not—think for one second that he had anything to do with that or any wrongdoing in any other case you may be dealing with now or in the future. Understood?"

"Sir, yes sir!" I said and gave a little salute.

"I'm glad we understand each other. Now, if there is nothing else, I need to finish tying this fly."

Dismissed. *Yes sir.* I headed for my desk. What if it was Judge Carson? What if that's Greta Bullfinch's secret?

And the next question: If he did, so what? What did that have to do with Maisie Gordon? Nothing. Probably. Maybe.

CHAPTER FORTY-SIX

T WAS AFTER TWO on Tuesday afternoon. I needed to see Greta Bullfinch. First, to apologize for Sheena's rude behavior when we accosted her outside Holy Assumption. I hoped she'd be in a forgiving mood.

Second, I hoped to convince her that she might have information important to the Gordon case. Maybe the raid on the strip club was related. Maybe the youngest Carson boy, William, a.k.a. Buddy, was Maisie's crush.

Whatever she knew, I hoped to persuade her to share it. And I'd persuade her in a kinder, gentler way than Sheena's bulldozer approach.

A fat bumblebee was visiting the climbing roses on Greta Bullfinch's front trellis as I approached. I rang the doorbell. No response. I rang again. Waited. Silence.

Sweat trickled down the back of my neck. I wiped my forehead with my palm. I hoped she was home. Maybe she'd invite me into the cool house, maybe offer me more lemonade.

I knocked and called out, "Miss Bullfinch? Greta? It's Mackenzie Prentice. May I speak with you please?"

Nothing. I took the sidewalk around to the back of the house. The sliding door was open. Not something you do on such a sweltering day.

My gut clenched.

I walked onto the deck, looked into the kitchen.

Greta Bullfinch was face down in the middle of the tile floor. Maybe she'd been outside in the garden, felt dizzy, came inside, and fainted. Maybe it was heat stroke.

I ran to her and saw a pool of blood forming under her head. I pressed my fingers on the side of her neck. Her pulse was faint but steady.

I patted my pockets. No cell phone. I'd left it in the car. *Damn!* I looked around the kitchen, saw the phone on the wall.

Just then I heard, "Holy crap! What happened?"

Sheena.

I yelled, "Call 911!"

"On it!" She held up her cell. "What's the address here?"

I told her. She made the call.

I got close to Greta's ear. "Help is coming. Hang on." Greta gave no sign that she heard me.

Sheena knelt next to me. "What the hell happened?"

"No idea. Maybe she was out in the heat, got dizzy, came inside for a glass of water, and fell. Hit her head?"

"Don't think so. Look at this." She shifted Greta's head slightly. A long slash along her cheek was oozing blood. A lot of blood. Sheena grabbed a kitchen towel and pressed it against the cut. "Knife wound. No question. Somebody cut her. Bad."

"A warning. Somebody wanted to shut her up," I said. Someone was determined to keep Greta Bullfinch from telling whatever secret it was she knew.

Sheena kept pressure on the cut. I held Greta's hand and bent to her ear. "Hang on, Greta. You'll be okay. Just hang on."

You say things like that, and you can only hope it turns out to be true.

FIFTEEN MINUTES LATER, I FOLLOWED THE ambulance in Cricket, and Sheena followed me in Trip's BMW. We parked in the hospital lot and waited in the emergency room. I lied and told the nurse that I was Greta's niece.

Greta's sister showed up. She was evidently Greta's emergency contact in the hospital system. The nurse at the desk pointed at us.

Greta's sister came over, squinted at me, suspicious. "You're not family. Who are you?"

"I'm Mackenzie, and this is Sheena. Friends of your sister's," I said. "I'm the one who found her." It was the simplest thing to say in the moment.

"Thank you! I'm her sister, Helga Anderson. Nice to meet you."

"Wish it was under better circumstances. I hope she's going to be okay," I said.

The nurse called Helga to sign something and then took her back to see Greta.

I explained to Sheena that this was Helga, the sister who was married to the brother of Gram's friend Velma, who told Gram, who told me, that Greta had a secret.

Sheena rolled her eyes. "Jesus, this is a small town." She went to get a coffee.

Five minutes later, Helga came back. "She's stitched up and resting. I'll stay here until she's ready to go home. Give me your number, and I'll let you know how she's doing."

I handed her my card.

Eyebrows up, she looked at me. "What? Investigations? What's this about?"

I explained who I really was and told her how my grandmother told me that Velma told her—well, the whole situation. "It's vital that I help get closure for Maisie Gordon's mother. She doesn't have much time left." I gave her an intense look. "If you know something, please tell me. Something your sister might have told you about the Carson family? A secret? A scandal, maybe?"

Her eyes got wide. "You think that had something to do with what happened today?"

Aha! Confirmation! There is *a secret something.* I nodded. "I'm pretty sure it's connected. Somebody may be giving your sister a warning."

"Those bastards," she said so quietly I barely caught it.

"What bastards?"

She looked at the floor, shook her head. "I'm sorry. It's not mine to tell. You'll have to talk to my sister." She stood. "I'm sorry. I'm going to sit with Greta."

She walked away.

Sheena came back. "Any progress? How's the old lady?"

I frowned. "Greta is her name, and she's an amazing older woman."

"Okay, whatever. Did you get anything from her?"

"Nope. Didn't wake up yet." I wasn't about to tell her what Helga had said. "I'm leaving now. I'll talk to Greta later."

"And I'll be there when you do," she said. Not asking permission. Stating a fact.

"Whatever," I said and headed outside to my car.

CHAPTER FORTY-SEVEN

Wednesday, July 3

NICK CALLED AS I drove to TriMak on Wednesday morning. He'd have the carriage house back to livable by the weekend. The tree branch had been removed and the roof sealed temporarily. He deemed the upstairs unsafe until all repairs could be made.

No access to my closet. No soft, poofy bed. No maple cathedral. No reading corner.

"Sorry it can't be sooner," Nick said and hung up. I felt a wave of relief that the damage wasn't worse. But meanwhile, I'd be staying in the Victorian, and borrowing clothes from my mother and grandmother. Again.

I poured out my frustration to Jimbo as I drove. "This is how it was after the apartment fire. I lost everything. I was homeless. And I—finally!—just moved on, and now this! I had *hope*, Jimbo. Hope!" I pounded the steering wheel and spewed every bad word I could think of.

Jimbo chirped sympathy. He evidently loves a good pity party.

In the middle of my spew, Helga Anderson called. Her sister was awake and wanted to talk to me.

Fifteen minutes later, I walked into Greta's hospital room. Officer Samantha Dutton was just leaving. She nodded to me.

"Good to see you, Officer," I said. Always good to be polite to people wearing guns.

"Same here, Prentice. Take care," she said.

Greta was sipping orange juice through a straw as Helga held the cup. Her right cheek was bandaged from her brows to her chin, and both eyes were bloodshot with darkening circles forming around each. Clear liquid ran from the plastic bag above her to the IV line attached to the back of her left hand.

Helga said, "She has a bad concussion. Her blood pressure's low, and she got about a million stitches. She's going to have a nasty scar. They admitted her last night because, well, her age, you know?"

Greta rolled her eyes. "That's enough, Helga. She doesn't need to know my whole medical history." She looked at me. "I want to talk to you."

Helga kept going. "They're doing more tests later. She might have a skull fracture. She might have a stroke. An aneurysm. A brain bleed." Her eyes got wide, her breath coming faster. "She might have seizures! Alzheimer's! Permanent brain damage!"

Nice to know that Anxious Me wasn't the only one who could spin out of control.

Greta used that teacher voice again and said, "Helga, that's enough! Calm down. Leave us alone." An order, not a request.

Helga took a breath. "Fine! I'll be right outside." As she passed me, she whispered, "Big sisters are so bossy."

I nodded. My big sister was bossy too. And evidently, judging from these two, that relationship dynamic lasts until the day we die.

I sat in the chair next to the bed and waited.

Greta reached for my hand, tears welling. "Thank you. If you hadn't come . . ." her voice trailed off.

I squeezed her hand. "I'm just glad I found you."

She wiped her eyes. "Can you raise this bed for me?"

I pressed the button, and the head of the bed rose. I adjusted her pillows.

"That's better. Thanks. Now, I need to know. Who would do this to me?"

"What do you remember?"

"I came home from a meeting at church and was in the kitchen. Someone grabbed me from behind. I felt a sharp pain in my face, and that's it. I woke up here. What happened?"

I paused, considering what to say next. "I don't know for sure, but it may have something to do with the Carsons and whatever that secret is you're protecting. And my guess is that it has something to do with Maisie Gordon's death."

She went paler than she already was and stared at the ceiling. I waited.

Finally, she folded her hands on her lap and looked at me, determination in her expression. "Well, then. Enough is enough. I'll tell you everything."

CHAPTER FORTY-EIGHT

I LEFT GRETA BULLFINCH, MULLING over what she'd told me. Major pieces of the puzzle were floating in my mind, but I couldn't quite put it all together. I needed proof to go to the police. Without proof, nothing could be done.

Meanwhile, I headed back to 3R cliff with Greg's metal detector and a wire coat hanger. I'd pulled the hanger straight and bent the end into a hook. I hoped what I'd seen wedged down in those rocks was Maisie's birthstone necklace.

Wind gusts buffeted Cricket as I drove across the Woodson Avenue Bridge. After a day of high temperatures and high humidity, an approaching cold front created perfect conditions for a storm. "Possibility of damaging winds," Stuart Klump had told us that morning. "Possibility of tornadoes in the viewing area. Stay tuned for updates."

I parked and checked the local weather app on my phone. The interactive map showed a huge line of thunderstorms coming from the west. The "future" feature on the map predicted the storm would hit Three Rivers within the hour.

The wind whipped my hair into my face as I walked the quarter mile to the "kinder, gentler" trail. I reached the riverbank and then made my way back along the shore to the rocks where Maisie died.

I paused, looking at the rocks again. Seeing the police photos of Maisie's body again, twisted, one bare arm, one bare foot. The poor kid.

I shook my head to clear the image, then climbed onto the rocks to the spot where I'd seen the whatever-it-was before. I illuminated the crevice with my cell flashlight as I extended the hanger hook toward the metal object. A few tries, and I snagged it and pulled it up.

It was a necklace with a silver cross, all right, but the thick chain held a heavy iron cross. Who lost it? Biker? Punk? Certainly not sweet, kitten-loving, fifteen-year-old Maisie.

I got up and stood at the edge of the water, looking up at the cliff.

If Maisie fell this way . . . I moved my hands in an arc. *Then maybe her necklace flew . . .* I pointed a dense clump of bullrushes to my right. Worth a shot.

I walked into the weeds with the metal detector, bending them to the side as I moved forward. Three feet in, the detector gave a faint beep. On my knees, I dug into the wet soil with my fingers. Several inches down, I felt metal and tugged.

A necklace on a silver chain. And on the chain, a cross with a stone in the middle.

I knelt there, closing my hand around the necklace. I believe there is something more than just this plane of existence. What it is, I can't say exactly.

But as I held the necklace, I sensed a connection. As if Maisie Gordon were standing behind me, smiling.

CHAPTER FORTY-NINE

RUBBED THE STONE IN the center of the cross against the leg of my shorts. The years of rain, snow, and dirt had pitted and discolored it, but it had to be Maisie's. After all, how many birthstone cross necklaces could there be lying near where a teenaged girl had died?

The clouds were getting darker by the second. The storm was coming, and Mrs. Gordon's time was almost up. I put the necklace in my pocket and scrambled up the quicker, steeper path to the cliff top, using the metal detector as a hiking pole.

Reaching the top, I rounded the buckthorn bushes that grew close to the edge. I leaned over to catch my breath.

"I'll take that."

I looked up. Charity Gordon.

I feigned ignorance. "What are you talking about?"

"The necklace. I watched you down there. I know you have it. Give it to me."

Lightning lit the western sky. I shouted over the thunder that followed. "I'm going to bring it to your mother!"

"No, you're not!"

"Why not?"

"Because it's not Maisie's. It's mine."

Ka-chunk! A big piece of the puzzle fell into place. I fingered the stone in my pocket. Not a ruby. Not Maisie's birthstone. Charity's birthstone. Topaz. "You were here with your sister that night," I said. Not a question. A fact.

"Yes, I was. I followed them up here. My brat of a sister lured him up here. My boyfriend! My Zach!"

Aha! B is for Boomer. Not Buddy. Not Jemma's Bubba. Not some mystery guy. Zachary "Boomer" Carson.

"Did you know that B with a heart on Maisie's mirror was *your* boyfriend?"

"Not at first. But I put two and two together." Charity sneered. "I caught her up here kissing him. The little slut!"

I ran the scene in my mind. Zach, Charity, and Maisie up here. Greta Bullfinch's secret. Greta, the housekeeper, had told me she found Zach Carson's football jersey in the hamper, dirty and bloody, the morning after Maisie died. She'd guessed that he had something to do with her death, and he admitted he was there. Greta kept silent. Loyalty to the family, she said.

"Zach killed her, didn't he, Charity?"

"Just give me the necklace." She took a step toward me.

I stepped back toward the cliff's edge. The chief's advice: keep them talking, try a soft approach. "That must have been so awful for you, seeing them like that."

Charity said, "I followed her up here. I just had a feeling about it all. You know?"

I'd had my suspicions about guys in the past. "Yeah, you just have a feeling. You know something's going on, even if you don't want to know."

"That's right." She got quiet.

I prompted her. "What happened then, Charity?"

"I got up here. Heard her saying how much she loved him. He had her on the ground. He was on *top* of her! I wasn't about to let that little brat ruin my chances with Zach." Charity looked off into the distance, replaying the movie in her head. "I screamed. He jumped up. I went after her. It was *her* fault he was up here."

Her voice rose, rage-filled, as she spat the next words. "That little brat always got everything she wanted. Everything!"

"So unfair," I said. *Keep her talking.* "Then what happened?"

"The three of us fought. I hit her. I choked her. She jumped over the rail. Said she was going to jump. I pushed her." Charity looked surprised at her own admission. As if acknowledging what she'd done for the first time. "Yes. I pushed her."

Confession is good for the soul, they say.

Charity continued. "I grabbed her by the sweatshirt, but she fell. I let go." She looked at me, eyes wide, innocent. "I had to let go, or I would have gone over with her. I had to."

I nodded. "It couldn't be helped. It was an accident."

She looked away again. "An accident, yes. An accident."

"What about Zach?"

Charity looked at me, disdain on her face. "Zach wanted to tell his daddy. Daddy, the judge, always bailed his boys out. No matter what they did. Underage drinking, stealing stuff." Her voice hardened. "But I told Zach if he told anyone—I mean, *anyone*—I'd say he was trying to rape her, and he'd go to jail. He was already eighteen. His daddy wouldn't have been able to get him out of a rape charge. He'd have lost his football scholarship, ruined his future. I made him swear we'd take it to our graves. And you know what? He started crying." She scoffed. "Crying! Can you imagine?"

Charity was one hard cookie.

She glared at me. "We've been just fine all these years. Nobody knew anything except that old lady housekeeper. And she wasn't talking—so loyal to the precious Carsons—until you came snooping around."

"You tried to kill her?"

She scoffed. "Not me! I'm a doctor, remember? 'Do no harm.' No, it was Zach. I told him to go over there and shut her up. I meant pay her off, but that idiot—" She came at me. "Give me that necklace!"

I pointed the metal detector at her, holding her off. I wasn't about to hand over the evidence that possibly incriminated her in her sister's death. Of course, she might argue that Maisie took it without her knowledge. Or that she lost it by the river some other time. But that would be up to a jury to decide.

I had to keep her talking while I figured out what to do. "How did your necklace end up down there?" I nodded toward the cliff.

Charity said, "It wasn't until after she fell that I realized she'd pulled my necklace off. I looked everywhere. I found hers on the ground up here, but not mine." Her eyes went cold as she came back to the present. "I've looked for that damn necklace so many times but never found it. Now I know why. Give it to me."

"If this is yours, then what did you do with Maisie's neck-lace? Why didn't you give it to your mother? She's wanted it all these years."

Her voice went soft again. "Maisie has it. I slipped it into her casket at the funeral. I never told my mother." Hard again, she demanded, "Give it to me. Now!"

Lightning cracked the sky, and the wind blew harder, colder. The storm was almost on us.

"One more question, Charity. What about the note? What did Maisie mean by 'It's all too much'?"

Charity laughed, a high-pitched, almost maniacal sound. "I forged that note! Copied her handwriting!" She glowered at me, then, the words coming in staccato. "I wanted my mother . . . to think her . . . precious . . . little darling . . . hated life so much that she jumped!"

How cruel could a daughter be? How uncaring. How jealous of a sibling. I shuddered. The wind came stronger as the first drops of cold rain pelted my arms. The metal of the guardrail was cold against the back of my knees.

I took a deep breath and shouted above the wind. "Charity, it's all over. You need to go to the police and tell them what happened."

"No way! There's no proof."

"You just confessed, and I'll swear to it."

"It's my word against yours. You're the only witness. You can have an accident too."

Charity lunged toward me and shoved me. Hard.

The metal detector flew from my hand as I fell backward over the railing, thumping my tailbone. Pain shot up my spine. I scrambled to my feet.

She grabbed the detector and swung it at me.

I dodged, stepping closer to the cliff edge. "Don't come any closer!"

"Or what?" A man's voice, loud, from behind Charity.

Zachary Carson had arrived.

Two against one now. Badass had been in this kind of situation before. When outnumbered and outweighed, talking is my biggest advantage.

I yelled over the howling wind. "Charity just told me how you tried to rape her sister!"

Zach shouted, "Liar!" Was he talking to me or to his wife?

Charity must have assumed she was the target. "I didn't tell her anything—just that we were here together that night!"

"Shut your damn mouth!"

"You shut yours!"

Ooh, husband-wife bickering. I tucked the necklace in my shorts pocket and hoped they wouldn't notice me taking a few quick steps toward the steep trail down to the river.

I'd almost reached the buckthorn patch when Zach intercepted me, grabbed me by the hair, and dragged me backward. *What a caveman. Ugh.*

Zach let go as Charity lunged at me again, got her hands around my throat, and started to squeeze.

I grabbed her shoulders and brought my knee up, hard, into her crotch. Girls may not have boy bits, but it still hurts to take a knee to the hoo-ha. She screamed and let me go.

Zachary took over, grabbing me from behind. "Give me the necklace!"

He bent my left arm back behind me and pulled my hand upward. *Say uncle? Not today, sucker.* Badass had joined the fight.

I stomped his right foot as I jammed my right elbow as hard as I could into his diaphragm.

He let out a groan as the air left his body. He let me go. High school football jock turned middle-aged marshmallow. Badass was relieved.

Charity had recovered. She came at me.

I was at the edge, facing the river, struggling for balance. *This is how it was for Maisie. And this is how it's going to be for me too.*

I focused on not looking down. I took the necklace out and held it above my head. "Back off, Charity or I'll throw it in the river. I swear, I will!"

Charity grabbed for the necklace.

I almost lost my balance. I windmilled my arms to keep from falling to the rocks below.

Charity snatched the necklace from my hand and started back over the guardrail.

She didn't make it. I turned in time to see someone leap over the rail and tackle her, knocking her down.

Sheena Shay.

Charity came up fast, and Sheena landed a right hook to her chin. Charity stumbled back. She dropped the necklace.

I scooped it up and shoved it back into my pocket.

Zach had caught his breath and joined the fight.

THE SCENE ROLLED LIKE A MOVIE in slow motion. The four of us, fighting on the edge of the cliff.

Lightning crackling. Thunder booming.

Sheena turns, swings at Zach. Misses.

Charity comes at me, aiming a fist to my face.

I dodge, stepping aside.

Charity is behind Sheena, trying to grab her hair.

Zach drives a fist toward Sheena.

Sheena ducks.

Zach's fist lands square, an uppercut into Charity's jaw.

Charity's expression changes to shock and awe as her head

snaps back, her eyes wide, her mouth forming a perfect "oh" as she loses her footing and starts to fall backward.

Zach reaches for her, misses, his shout of "Nooooo!" drowned by the thunder.

The sky opens, rain pummels the three of us—Sheena, Zach, and me—as we stand, helpless, watching Charity's body falling, falling as her scream echoes up the cliff.

The crunch of bones breaking as her body hits the rocks below, lost in the cacophony of the storm.

CHAPTER FIFTY

TIME SEEMED SUSPENDED AS rain soaked my hair, my shirt, my shorts, and my shoes. Thoughts came slowly. *Someone should go down there. Someone should see if Charity is still breathing.* I felt numb, frozen in place.

I snapped back to reality as Sheena hollered my name. She and Zach were still trading punches, swearing at each other as they slipped around in the mud.

Sheena is one tough mudder. Badass was impressed.

I jumped over the guardrail to join the fight just as Sheena bent over and ran at Zach, ramming her head into his gut. He wrapped his arms around her mid-section and hoisted her up, holding her upside down. She faced the cliff, her head at his knees and her knees at his ears. It seemed all his football-playing strength had returned.

He howled a litany of curse words as he carried Sheena upside down over the guardrail— toward the edge of the cliff.

I jumped onto his back, grabbed him by the hair. "Let her go!" I screamed into his ear.

"No! Don't!" Sheena screeched.

Zach gave a roar and tossed Sheena away. She rolled in the mud to the very edge of the cliff.

Then she went over.

"You bastard!" I screamed as I pounded his ears with my fists.

He reached back, grabbed my face, and dug his fingers into my eye sockets. I yelped and jumped off his back.

Zachary Carson stopped, looked at the river, and then looked at me. *What?* He was crying. He'd evidently had enough. He blubbered something as he ran toward the path to the parking lot. I didn't try to stop him.

I heard Sheena screaming my name. I ran to the cliff edge.

Sheena clung to a rock with one white-knuckled hand. The other hand clutched a clump of buckthorn—the "devil weed"—as she dangled over the edge.

"Help me! For the love of God, pull me up!"

I grabbed her by the forearms and pulled. She pushed against the cliff face with her feet. She wrapped one hand around my wrist, then the other. I pulled harder.

The rain pelted us. The mud and rocks at the cliff edge got slipperier by the second.

"Don't let go!" Sheena screamed, sheer terror on her face.

Did she honestly think I'd let her fall? I swear I had not for one second pictured her going off that cliff. Not for one second did I imagine how easy it would be to let her go. Not. One. Second.

Okay, maybe one.

"I've got you, Sheena," I screamed.

Adrenaline surged. I sat down in the mud, braced my heels against the rocks on the cliff edge.

I pushed against the rocks, scooted back an inch, and pulled. Push, scoot, pull. Again. Push, scoot, pull. (Thank you, Sully's Gym and that accursed leg press machine.)

One last pull with all my strength, and Sheena Shay was back on the top of the cliff, lying on my legs, her face in my crotch.

I felt like I'd just given birth to a really bitchy baby.

She rolled off me. We lay there, bloody, beaten, filthy, and soaked to the skin, on our backs in the storm. The rain poured down, the clouds roiled, black and ominous, as the tornado sirens in town blasted a warning.

Then Sheena started laughing.

And then, so did I.

A second later, we were both crying.

CHAPTER FIFTY-ONE

HE TORNADO SIRENS SCREAMED on, joined by emergency vehicle sirens. Police officers and EMTs in rain gear crested the hill, Detective Heather Sullivan among them.

I looked at Sheena as we sat up. "You called the cops?"

She held her jaw and grimaced as she nodded. "Yeth, I did."

The EMTs checked us over while I gave Heather a quick summary. She ordered people down to the riverbank.

"We arrested Zachary Carson fleeing the scene," she said. "Says you killed his wife. Did you?"

The look I shot her answered her question.

"Fine," she said. "I'll need your statement in the morning."

"No problem." I took the necklace from my pocket. "You'll want this. I found it in the bushes down there. It's Charity Gordon's. She lost it the night she pushed her sister off the cliff."

Heather yelled over the noise of the storm. "Somebody bring me an evidence bag." Small detective. Big voice. One of her minions came running.

I wished I had minions.

The rain had subsided just as the chief, Trip, and Germany arrived.

Trip grabbed Sheena. She yowled and held her jaw. "Ith broken! I know ith broken!"

An EMT confirmed that. Trip said he'd take her to the hospital, then escorted her away.

The chief hugged my shoulders. "We've got to stop meeting like this, Chickie."

Heather came over to tell me that officers at the riverbank confirmed that Charity Gordon was dead. I wobbled a little.

The chief held me at arm's length, looked me over. "You okay?"

My ribs hurt, and my arms ached. My backside had taken a thumping. "I'm fine," I said.

Germany looked concerned. "Are you sure?"

I nodded. "Yeah, kid. I'm fine." The wind whipped my hair. Several wet strands got stuck in my mouth.

Chief Bronson pushed them off my face, kept his palm against my cheek for a moment. Kind. Fatherly.

I blinked back tears.

The chief looked at me another long moment, then said, his voice gentle, "Seriously, you have to learn to call for backup."

Germany heard that. "Yeah, you should have called me. I would have been here for you!"

"Next time, Foghorn. Next time," I said. It hurt to smile, but I managed.

The necklace secured, Charity dead, Zach arrested, and Sheena rescued, it was my turn to fall apart. I started to shake.

The chief held me until I calmed, then escorted me down the long, long path to my car. He gave Cricket's keys to Germany, told him to follow us to Gram's, and insisted on driving me home.

I didn't protest.

CHAPTER FIFTY-TWO

Thursday, July 4

THURSDAY MORNING, THE FOURTH of July, dawned dry and sunny. The storm had passed. Stuart Klump predicted a perfect day, with low humidity and temperatures in the low seventies. The kind of perfect summer day we live for here.

Fourth of July. Maisie Gordon's birthday. *Happy Birthday, Maisie. We know what happened to you, now. I'm so sorry. So, so sorry.* A sense of peace washed over me, as if Maisie were letting me know she was free now. Like I said, I don't believe in ghosts, but I smiled at the thought.

Gram and Nathan were having breakfast in the kitchen when I came downstairs. I assumed my mother was at Duncan's. I'd raided her closet for a pair of shorts and a Three Rivers Marathon tee shirt.

Gram looked adorable in her tee shirt with red and white stripes. Her blue shorts were covered in little white stars. She said, "The tornado went north of here. I heard it on the radio.

Some property damage but nobody hurt, thank the good Lord." She looked hard at me. "Are you okay?"

I gave her the executive summary of the case and the events on the cliff. "I just have a few bumps and bruises. I'm fine, but Sheena Shay isn't. And Charity Gordon Carson certainly is not."

She shook her head. "Oh goodness, goodness! You could have been killed. That tornado might have hit while you were up on that cliff." She put a hand to her heart. "Oh, dear God! Thank you, Jesus!"

Nathan said, "Did I ever tell you about the tornado I was in?"

Gram patted his hand. "Eat your eggs, dear, before they get cold."

Nathan dug into his breakfast.

I told them I'd meet them at the park for the family picnic later.

I wanted to check on Sheena. The chief called my cell as I drove to Our Lady of Mercy.

"Damnedest thing," he said. "After that mess on the cliff, I got to thinking about the strip club raid. I talked to Rollo Carson this morning. Asked him point blank. All three of his boys were at the strip club the night of the raid. They'd been doing all kinds of stuff there, he said. The youngest, Buddy, was still a minor. Rollo admitted he was the one who tipped them off. Didn't want them getting arrested." He paused. "Damn. He asked me if I could understand. How the hell does he expect me to understand something like that?"

"I'm so sorry, Chief. I know you and the judge are good friends."

He paused. "Yeah, I thought we were, but this? I'll never understand it. Damnedest thing." He hung up.

Rollo Carson, "pillar" of the Three Rivers community. Maybe that kind of pressure gets to you. Maintaining that image of the perfect life, perfect family living on the high hill. What happens when it's threatened? People do stupid things. I hoped the chief would be able to forgive his old friend.

Sheena was napping when I got to her room.

I touched her on the shoulder, and she opened her eyes. Her face was swollen and discolored on the left side. She tried to talk but couldn't. She grabbed a pen and a paper pad from the bed table across her lap, wrote something, and handed it to me.

THANK YOU.

"You're welcome." I pointed at her face. "Painful, huh?"

She groaned and nodded. She looked like she had plenty more to say but sighed and slumped back against her pillows.

"You look tired. I'll let you rest."

She nodded, tried to smile but stopped. Shook her head, then reached for my hand. She squeezed it. Tears filled her eyes.

I cleared my throat. Vulnerable Sheena I was not prepared for. "It's okay," I said. "You'll be fine. We'll be back to catching bad guys in no time."

She let go of my hand and made a noise. Might have been a laugh. Or maybe it was gas. Hard to tell with babies.

I ran into Trip and Germany as I headed for the elevator.

Germany said, "Hey, Mack. Did Sheena tell you?"

"How could she? She can't talk."

He said, "Oh, right. Well, we're staying in Three Rivers for a while. Gonna be working with you guys. Isn't that great?"

Working with Germany would be okay. But Sheena? Not so much.

"Trip? What's the deal? We're partners. Seems like this should be a group decision—you, me, and the chief."

"I guess, uh, I just made an executive decision. Sorry." He shrugged. "Easier to ask forgiveness than permission, right?"

I gave him a long look. He'd probably done that a lot, growing up with his domineering, controlling father. "I'm not sure about this. It's a big change."

Trip said, "You're right. You're right. I should have asked you and the chief. But how can we send her away when she's got a broken jaw? Injured in the line of duty. And on our case."

Germany piped up. "I can help run the office. You'll be licensed and will need more freedom to be out there. Foghorn, your faithful sidekick, will be taking care of things for you."

That certainly had some appeal. And Sheena had jumped into the fray on the cliff. I looked at Germany and then at Trip. They both had that can-we-please-keep-the-puppy look. I was too tired to argue. "Fine, whatever," I said.

I left them, took the elevator to the lobby, and found my way to Mrs. Gordon's room.

She was deep into a morphine-induced dream. The nurse left me with her, whispering on the way out, "It won't be long now."

People say they want the truth but then don't like what you have to tell them.

Mrs. Gordon gave no sign that she heard me as I assured her that Maisie never would have wanted to leave her mother or her cats. That was the truth.

"She wrote that note about school, too much homework. Definitely not a good-bye note."

I told her that Maisie had gone off the cliff by accident, probably carried over by a strong gust of wind.

I told her I'd found Maisie's necklace. "I'll make sure it goes with you," I said. Big fat lies, all of that.

I squeezed Mrs. Gordon's hand and thanked her, told her how grateful I was that she'd asked me to find out what happened.

I didn't like the truth I found, but I was grateful I'd found it.

As I turned to leave, Maisie's grandfather rolled into the room with Ferguson behind him. He said over his shoulder, "Leave us." Ferguson did an about-face and left to stand guard outside the door.

The old man looked me up and down. "You resolved this matter, Ms. Prentice?"

I nodded. "Yes, sir."

"I've spoken with the police. I'm, uh, sorry—" The general was obviously not accustomed to apologizing. "I'm sorry if my granddaughter, Charity, or that husband of hers caused you harm."

"I'm very sorry about Charity, sir."

He shook his head. "I've never understood her. She had all the advantages. I provided for them all. I paid for Charity's medical school. Still so ungrateful, so self-absorbed, so entitled. It's unfortunate, but I understand what happened to her couldn't have been prevented. You bear no responsibility for that."

"Thank you, sir. I appreciate that."

"I overheard what you told my daughter just now. Kind of you to withhold the facts under these circumstances. She doesn't have much longer." The general blinked hard and looked away, cleared his throat.

He'd lost his wife, son-in-law, two grandchildren, and soon his daughter would be gone. I couldn't begin to fathom the depth of a grief like that. I didn't know what to say, so I said nothing.

After a moment he cleared his throat and looked at me. Back to business. "Since you are the one who resolved this entire matter, I'm not sure why I should be paying Ms. Shay."

I swear I did not, for one second, think about throwing Sheena under the bus.

Well, maybe for one second.

But then, in a moment of unprecedented generosity, I said, "It was a team effort, sir. Sheena was instrumental in this case. I could not have resolved it without her. Or her assistant, Germany." I hoped he didn't notice my nose growing.

I turned to leave, then remembered something. "Sir, in my investigation, I came across some letters in Maisie's room. Letters from her grandmother Margaret. Your wife, I assume?"

I heard his sharp intake of breath. "My wife, yes. Where are the letters?"

"In Maisie's desk drawer in her bedroom."

He reached for my hand. "Thank you, Ms. Prentice. Thank you. You've been, uh, most kind." He let go and called Ferguson, who came in and wheeled him to his daughter's bed for a final goodbye.

When I got to the parking lot, Nick was standing by my car, looking worried. He hugged me and whispered into my hair. "Your grandmother told me what happened last night. Are you okay?"

"Bruised and battered, but nothing's broken."

Relief swept his face. "Thank God," he said. He took both my hands in his and met my eyes. "What do you say we watch the fireworks together later? I could pick you up at, say, eight? Unless, of course, you have other plans."

I smiled. "I'd love to watch the fireworks with you, Nick. I'll bring snacks and the cooler."

"No need. I'll take care of all that. And I'll bring the lawn chairs."

"I'd prefer a blanket," I said. Lonely Me had all kinds of ideas about that.

"A blanket it is, then." He smiled.

We like his smile. A lot.

He kissed me. And I kissed him back.

We like kissing Nick. All the parts of me agreed.

I watched him walk away.

Mm, mm, mmmm. Looking forward to the fireworks.

COMING SOON: Book Five in the Series

OLD HABITS

A Mackenzie Prentice Mystery

She screamed, and her shriek echoed up the bell tower, but until the bells rang on Sunday, no one would know what happened to Sister Mary Agnes.

ALL HALLOWS' EVE APPROACHES, and Three Rivers is abuzz with activity. The town loves Halloween, with the decorations and the bonfire. And this year's Halloween parade is set to be the biggest extravaganza ever. Staff and students at Holy Assumption Academy have been fundraising all year for a new gymnasium. Their Halloween Fright Night is going to be the culminating event, putting them over the top of their fundraising goal. At least, that's the hope.

Mackenzie Prentice is thirty-five, has a touch of OCD, is addicted to sugar, may occasionally drink too much, and has those voices in her head commenting on her choices. In this fifth book of the Mackenzie Prentice Mysteries, Mack goes undercover with Chief Bronson to solve a nun's murder. Mack realizes she has demons of her own to exorcise as she stumbles along an endless labyrinth of missteps and dead ends, following a trail that is, at times, as cold as a sepulchre.

ACKNOWLEDGMENTS

THANKS TO YOU FIRST, DEAR READER, for spending some of your precious time in Three Rivers with Mackenzie and the gang. You keep reading, and I'll keep writing.

Thank you, Michelle Rayburn (missionandmedia.com) for cheerleading, editing, designing, and consulting. You are a leader in this new indie publishing paradigm, and you are simply the best.

Thank you to Joe Coughlin for so generously sharing his expertise and experiences in law enforcement. (Errors in that area are strictly my own.)

Thanks to my dear sister Carol for the laughter we've shared. Thanks to the family clan: Alex, Katy, Lizz, Jenny, Laura, Dan, partners, and offspring—so grateful to have you all. And thanks to the real-life Joey, Charlie, and Violet for inspiring the characters. A special shout-out to Kiley for the birthstone necklace inspiration.

Thanks to my fellow Substack writers, who inspire me with their love of language and vulnerability. I draw inspiration—and courage—from all of you.

To readers: Maureen, Dan, Kelly, Janis, Melyssa, Fern, Lindy, Laura, Paula, Mary Lee, Jane, Nancy, Liz, Jessie, Deirdre, Ashley, Barbara, and Mack's other fans, thank you for your enthusiasm in spreading the word.

Finally, thank you to my darling Terry for forty years of love and encouragement. The best jokes have always been from you.

ABOUT THE AUTHOR

MARY PIERCE IS THE AUTHOR OF the Mackenzie Prentice Mysteries, a lifelong dream. She is also the author of three books of humorous inspiration / memoir published by Harper Collins/Zondervan: *When Did I Stop Being Barbie and Become Mrs. Potato Head*; *Confessions of a Prayer Wimp*; and *When Did My Life Become a Game of Twister*; along with hundreds of articles and a humor column for a national magazine.

Mary spent twenty years as a keynote humorist, bringing laughter and encouragement to audiences at women's wellness events and retreats around the country.

She left the speaking circuit to care for her aging mother, who had dementia. After six years as primary family caregiver, Mary returned to school, earning a master's degree in Clinical Mental Health Counseling at the age of sixty. As a licensed psychotherapist, she works with adults who are dealing with depression, anxiety, and life changes, specializing in trauma reprocessing and support for family caregivers.

Mary enjoys sketching, art journaling, and messing around with collage and assemblage as a mixed media artist. (What is it about fingers full of paint and glue that brings such joy?)

She and her husband, Terry, share six children and eleven grandchildren. They make their home in Wisconsin, with Sammy, a goldendoodle named after their favorite pizza place.

You can find Mary on Substack: *Old Woman, New Life by Mary Pierce* at www.marypierce.substack.com.

www.ingramcontent.com/pod-product-compliance
Lightning Source LLC
Chambersburg PA
CBHW020618260626
47157CB00003B/1067